DON'T CLEAN THE AQUARIUM

AND OTHER TALES OF HORROR

by JEFFREY OSIER

The centerpiece of our world was that great, all-encompassing tree. Not only did it seem to be the most gigantic living thing in all creation, but I was convinced that it was truly conscious of my presence, and of my almost constant need for reassurance. It was warm to the touch in the same way my parents were warm to the touch—a purposeful, protective radiation. Did I say it was the centerpiece of our world? No, that isn't quite true. Because it bathed me in its radiance, I was sure, as I had never been and as I would never be again, that I was the centerpiece of the world. My parents had always treated me as though I were the single most significant part of their lives, but I was beginning to sense their occasional distraction, their irritation. The tree seemed to care for nothing but me, and recognized and magnified my importance.

We loved to play beneath the tree, to bathe in the sunlight it filtered upon us, to climb those accommodating branches. We would search out its soft, moist places, where we would rest our palms, our cheeks, and listen for those intoxicating atmospheric disturbances that were beyond mere sound. And it was high in those branches that the world of our parents and all the pains and failures that filled our fragile little lives faded out of existence. The tree was the world, its branches the continents, its leaves the oceans and we … its attendant angels.

CONTENTS

Don't Clean The Aquarium!	1
The Shabbie People	28
The Big Ol' Clown Lady	50
The Hive	62
Radio Glossolalia	78
Snowligh.	89
Tiny Islands	111
Horizon Line	141

Author's Introduction

I spent most of the eighties working as an animator, fathering two adorable children, and in general just trying not to be such a teenager as I entered my thirties. During this time, I was an *extremely* failed science-fiction writer, in that I was a prolific short story writer who read widely in the field but never sold anything and really considered it a victory just to get a personal rejection from any editor who went so far as to read the story. Truth is, I was not very good. From the years 1980 to 1986, I went from weak Michael Bishop-like pastiches to weak Lucius Shepard pastiches with occasional clueless diversions into cyberpunk (which felt kind of funny in that I didn't even own a computer yet).

In November 1986, one of my animation cohorts asked me if I'd ever written a horror story. A good friend of his was launching a small press horror fiction magazine. I was only vaguely aware that such things existed, and I had never so much as held one in my hand.

The last thing I could remember writing that qualified as a horror story was a surreal little lump of poison called Catalog, from the spring of '78, dreamt up after too much Ballard, too many acid flashbacks, and way too impressionable a first viewing of Eraserhead. It was still lodged firmly in a spiral notebook, in a box, in the basement. I fished it out, read it, decided it was too off the wall for what I thought this editor would be looking for, went upstairs, opened the spiral notebook I was currently filling, and started writing what would turn out to be my first published short story. It was actually quite easy. The story was something that anybody who'd ever known me would have recognized as my work immediately. It was me, through and through, in a way no science fiction I'd ever written could even compare. I was very proud of that story. I typed it up and handed it off to my friend at work who handed it off to his friend the fledgling magazine editor. That story was "Encyclopedia for Boys" and the editor was Mark Rainey, who was putting together the first issue of his magazine Deathrealm.

Not really sure whether he would accept it or not, I immediately leaped into another project that had occurred to me while writing that first story. While I was writing it, I was having a lot of dreams, some of them veering into nightmare, about fish and aquariums. I was, at that time, having some issues with my own aquarium, and the dreams were spectacular, wide-screen magnifications of what, in truth, were just some laziness-caused maintenance issues. Often, I was wandering a labyrinth where all the walls were aquarium glass, so that I was surrounded by gigantic masses of water and huge, unfamiliar fish. Somehow, my aquarium issues and the dreams they inspired, led me to the idea that ended up as my second published story, "Don't Clean the Aquarium."

At this point, my lifetime's reading of horror fiction consisted of the following: Poe and Matheson in junior high, Lovecraft in high school, and just a few months previously, one of the Clive Barker Books of Blood (the one with "Rawhead Rex"). I had yet to read Stephen King or Peter Straub or Ramsey Campbell or Robert McCammon, let alone anyone from that entire subculture of small press horror writers, into whose midst I was about to be pooted.

Reading "Don't Clean the Aquarium" today, it's obvious that what I was really trying to evoke was some kind of Roger Corman movie from 1958, with Dick Miller as the protagonist and an amazing, on-the-cheap Paul Blaisdell monster in the aquarium. Wouldn't that have been great? Anyway, my point is that "Don't Clean the Aquarium" is the last un-self-conscious horror story I ever wrote. I didn't write it for an audience. I wasn't even sure I was going to type it up once I was finished with the longhand version. It was just me and my influences and my dreams poured into the claustrophobic corridors of those damned, fine-line, green-tinted spiral notebooks. Luckily, my first story had been fairly well-received in that first issue of *Deathrealm*, so Mark was expressing interest in my next story. So I typed it up and it appeared in *Deathrealm #2*, complete with my illustration of the aquarium beast, which, true to the times, was more Giger than Blaisdell.

But the thing you people will never appreciate about "Don't Clean the Aquarium" is just how lovely and magnificent an example of penmanship the original version was.

Rereading "The Shabbie People" now, I wish I could take one last walk down Lower Wacker Drive the way it once was… the way it still was when I wrote the story in the fall of 1990. Here were the underbellies of the skyscrapers along Wacker Drive proper, full of decay and recesses so dark and dank that they sometimes seemed almost otherworldly, or at least, a portal to an underworld. Or so my warped imagination used to tell me as I walked from the train to work along Lower Wacker nearly every morning for about five years. It wasn't a true underground: the lower drive had its share of traffic, and in most places you could clearly see the tour boats on the Chicago River. Especially in winter, homeless people built shelters near the heating vents of the skyscrapers. By the time I wrote this story in October of 1990, Lower Wacker was no longer anywhere near my train or office. I was going through a divorce, grappling with the complexities of a new relationship, living in a cold, sterile apartment that I could not adjust to, when I sat down to write this story whose idea had occurred to me a couple of years before, when my circumstances – and reasons for wanting to write the story – had been far different. "The Shabbie People" was supposed to be about something other than isloation and loneliness and the choking inability to make meaningful human connection, The story I actually wrote was ultimately overwhelmed by my unhappiness and fear of the future, so it ended up being about the state of the author writing it and not about what it was supposed to be about, which was something to do with shy sentinels from some other realm and the strange, tentative interactions they have with their near-relatives (or near-analogs, at any rate), human beings. This story first appeared in a fine anthology edited by George Hatch, *Souls in Pawn*.

Much as I like this story, it has always bothered me because, as you may have already figured out, I can't read it without being overwhelmed by the circumstances under which I wrote it. But George liked it, and it was subsequently reprinted in Karl Edward Wagner's *Years Best Horror XXI*, one of two stories I placed in that year's anthology.

Of course, if you drive or walk Lower Wacker today, you'll wonder what all the fuss was about. Sealed up in concrete and reassuringly well-lit, it is as cold and lifeless a place as that apartment I wrote the story in. It's probably safer in every practical way imaginable, but I prefer to think of it as I remember it in my damaged, desperate early thirties: a decaying underground neighborhood, festering under a soft green glow, a world of recesses and portals, of car exhaust and the vented breaths of the office buildings atop it. It was a calming place to take a walk in those days. And you always had good company in your solitude.

One weekend in 1987, while I was driving through rural Wisconsin with my wife and three-year-old daughter, we passed something that I can still picture vividly to this day. Or at least, can pretend to remember vividly. Truth is, we passed it very quickly and my impression of the place had to be pieced together afterwards from the blurring scraps I actually saw. It was a black tanker, like from a truck or maybe a train (I had only a second or two to process this, remember). It had a door, cheerfully trimmed with something colorful, and it was fronted by a lush, beautiful garden. What the hell? I never saw it again (at the time we were lost and trying to find our way back to our intended route).

Meanwhile, my office-mate and I, animators both, had taken to bestowing names to people around the office we didn't actually know. Since we were freelancers, not actual employees, and had low status around the office, these names were very important to us. There was Squeaks, the Real Norman Bates, the Little Skull Girl, and the Big Ol' Clown Lady. The latter was a cranky older woman who worked a register at the pharmacy where we sometimes bought our afternoon sustenance. She was large, unkempt, had big, suspicious eyes she surrounded in a forbidding mascarascape, and wore bright, violently applied red makeup on not-quite random sections of her face. We only ever saw her two or three times, but she was memorable enough to get a name, and memorable enough to miss once she disappeared. The name, too good to let go to waste, had to be good for something.

Also very important was the fact that for the past few years I'd been working on a series of educational films about body systems: the digestive system, the nervous system, the heart, the respiratory system, the kidneys, the immune system, etc, etc. I was now writing the films, working on the animation during film production, and editing the film and sound afterwards. I'd had it up to *here* with the human body and all it's organy, easily malfunctioning machinery. Particularly important to "The Big Ol' Clown Lady" were the medical paintings of F. Netter, to which we referred frequently while designing animation of the human interior. No one could paint a diseased organ like F. Netter. And no matter what we were researching, it was always the pictures of diseased organs that we came to rest on. In fact, the single most common reprimand around our office was "Stop looking at pictures of diseased organs!"

So there you have it: Barely glimpsed oil tank with a door and a lush garden PLUS scary lady who's mean to us when we buy our afternoon candy PLUS painting of diseased organs from anatomy texts EQUALS The Big Ol' Clown Lady. That's how easy it is to be me.

Even while I was writing this story, I knew that I wanted to sell it to Peggy Nadramia's *Grue Magazine*, which I was very enthusiastic about at the time. It ended up being my only appearance in *Grue*. It's appearance there was significant in another way: the illustration for my story was by one H. E. Fassl, who would later surface in my actual real life as Harry Fassl, a great friend who passed away in 2008.

"The Hive" was a stand-alone story I wrote as a 'proof of concept' for a novel idea I had in the mid-90s. I was newly remarried, working a much more high pressure job than I'd ever had before, and I had stopped writing and submitting horror stories a couple of years previously. I was now in my early forties and it seemed to me that I was going through great changes, the kind of changes that cast fresh light and scrutiny on the priorities of the past. I was trying to write a novel while grappling with the feeling that I might not want to be a novelist as much as I had once believed I did. As a result, I never even finished a first draft of the novel, but in the meantime I worked on the freestanding version of "The Hive," which in its imagery, its ridiculous setting, and its bitter, anti-family subtext, seemed a reasonably saleable horror story in the vein I was now known for.

Reading it now, I'm drawn back in to that gigantic, grotesque, and impossible wooden structure and the family that may or may not have built it, but who protected it and many of whom lived and died in it. The novel was supposed to be the unraveling of all the secrets that explained why it was there and why the people in it behaved as they did. I can still remember what the place looked and smelled like, as well as the subtleties of feature that were visible in one form or another on the faces of every member of that bloodline. And of course I know the entire secret behind the family and their Hive. But when I read the story now, and recollect the backstory I had conjured up, it all seems so mundane and trite. Hardly implausible by the standards of the modern horror novel (I can't believe I just wrote that), but vastly inferior to the mystery it was explaining. It points out one of my key weaknesses as a proto-horror-novelist: my ideas were best presented in short-story or (especially) novella form, and every time I tried to write a horror novel, my ideas got rammed and scraped and gouged into things I did not intend, and did not like. I wasn't actually a big enough fan of the horror novels I'd read to have any desirable models to aspire to, and I wasn't stubborn enough to write a novel that was wholly as weird as one of my stories. I never salvaged much from the two unpublished horror novels I finished in 1992 and 1993, but I'm glad I salvaged "The Hive" from my unfinished one, and especially glad that Mark Rainey picked it up for *Deathrealm*, my last appearance in that magazine.

In 1988, during the period when I was producing my greatest number of horror stories, I once either heard or read the word *glossolalia* somewhere. It was such a mellifluous-sounding word, yet even in context I had no idea what it meant. However, the moment I looked it up (it means speaking in tongues), I got the idea for "Radio Glossolalia," about a station that only broadcasts a single voice speaking in tongues. It is only on late at night, and never at the same frequency. At the time I was writing stories that could easily be interpreted as descent into madness but which were told literally and bluntly enough that they were presented as slightly overheated reportage. Eddie may doubt his own sanity, but the narrator never has any doubts. Eddie is sane and alert, and this is all really happening. In this and also in the way it plays out plot-wise, this story is very similar to another story of mine, "The Little Skull Girl," although I believe "Radio Glossolalia" to be the more effective of the two. Most of my best stories were actually novellas, and few of my shorter works compared with the best of my novellas. This one did. It appeared in *Noctulpa #4*, edited by George Hatch. George was a great hands-on editor for this and for "The Shabbie People," asking a lot of good questions and helping me to focus on a couple of notable improvements.

I wrote "Snowlight" in March of 1987, in the month before my son Greg was born and a little more than 20 years after the events described in that story. I was about to become a father and at the same time grappling yet again, and as awkwardly as ever, with my memories of the death of my own father, when I was 12 years old and living in Hillside, Illinois. I had been a small, dreamy, and defenseless little kid who did nothing but draw pictures, watch movies, and read monster magazines, and the transition to adolescence was already explosive enough. The chain reaction of anger, disillusionment, and depression my father's death set off in my family engulfed me completely, and I was to spend the next three-and-a-half years in a kind of stupor, all the while desperately and ineptly trying to disguise myself as a normal kid. "Snowlight" takes place during those weeks when I first fell into that stupor over my last few months of seventh grade. The story is probably about 90 percent true. The skitching, the house that burned down, the snowball attack, the angry driver who chased me through a field – all that is true. The other ten percent should be pretty easy to spot. It seemed to me at the time that writing this story was a major catharsis in my life, and a great symbolic gesture at the birth of my son and the twentieth anniversary of my father's death. A nice sentiment, I'm sure, but I remember the intent more than any catharsis it might have caused me. I did draw a smashing cover piece for *Deathrealm #4*, the issue in which "Snowlight" appeared: a portrait of the irate driver in a much happier mood.

If "Snowlight" represented the beginning of my descent into the stupor, "Tiny Islands," which takes place in the summer of my sixteenth birthday, 1970, represents my reawakening. I fell in love for the first time (with not even a hint of success the whole while), started writing and drawing again, started playing guitar, completely altered my reading habits. I now wanted to write a sequel to "Snowlight," something that showed Danny Pickett, my alter ego, going through a similar reawakening. This story takes place in a town vaguely similar to the town I went to high school in, Naperville, IL, where we all swam at an old quarry that had been converted into a large, algae-friendly swimming pool and poked around on a couple of nearby tiny islands in the the DuPage River. I wrote this story during the turbulent spring of 1990, as my first marriage collapsed. It seemed strangely sweet and wholesome to me at the time, and it was not until years later that I read this story and realized... I hate all these kids. Especially Danny Pickett. I hope to hell I was never actually like this, though I suspect that, being so much closer to those ages when I wrote those stories, I knew what I was talking about.

There was to be a third story about Danny Pickett, about the events leading up to his dropping out of college. I may have even started it, but I never got very far and I suspect the manuscript is lost forever. In thinking back on it now, I fear that what I was really trying to do in that story was explain what was really going on in the first two Danny Pickett stories. Whatever kind of rationalization I may have come up with to tie "Snowlight" and "Tiny Islands" together, not even I can remember now. Luckily.

The final story in this volume, "Horizon Line," was written in November and December 1993. I was losing focus as a horror writer now, having abandoned a highly marked up second draft of my second horror novel in frustration and disgust. I had no market in mind for this story. Rather, I wrote it for a live reading at the Red Lion Pub in Lincoln Park that December. As a result, I began reading it out loud while it was still in first draft, and by the time I read it publicly, I'd already read it out loud more than a dozen times. The lone character on the atoll was something I'd been carrying with me for years and had been part of several earlier, much less successful stories. A lot of Ballard and Conrad went into the long gestation of this idea, but when I finally sat down to write it, the book that most influenced me was a short work about the Aztecs, *This Tree Grows In Hell* by Ptolemy Tompkins. I was unhinged and alone and lonely and that twisted little goblin of a book, which seemed to obsess more horrifically on its subject than anything I'd ever read on the Aztecs, cast a gloom over me that ate through all the blue skies and ocean vistas my character saw on that atoll. I was going through a lot of changes during this time, and these changes would continue, and even accelerate, over the next year. What I didn't realize at this time was that I was finally starting to come out of a funk that had dogged me most of my life. But at the time, this transitional life I was living seemed bleak and hopeless. I felt so doomed, and I spent so much time alone, letting all the rot of my past bubble to the surface in my many hours alone in my dark and dingy garden apartment. I didn't intend for "Horizon Line" to be such a stark confessional, and it's odd to read it now and realize that the character's confession bore no relation at all to my own life. But the fear, humiliation, bitterness, and crushing loneliness he feels were my own, and the rebirth he hopes to experience was what I too was banking on. Of course nothing I tried to trigger that rebirth helped, and when it finally did happen it was at a most unexpected moment and not at all what I had pictured.

More than any other story in this volume, "Horizon Line" is about the conditions and circumstances under which I wrote it. And in that final scene, it's obvious (to me anyway) that the narrator is much more anxious to move on than the main character is. He's pushing the main character towards the exit door because that's where he himself is headed.

Jeff Osier
April 10, 2011

DON'T CLEAN THE AQUARIUM!

As I write this, I can't help but imagine you—my readers, going through my narrative, shaking your heads in disgust and saying, whenever I reach a moment of crisis, "Well, this guy had it coming to him." I can hear you mumbling away through my tribulations with the smug assurance that you don't and obviously couldn't have my problems, and that, well, I should probably have never kept pets, anyway. Not that I could keep them.

And it's not that I'm purposely setting out to evoke sympathy. I really couldn't care less. By the time anyone reads this it will be too late for it to make any real difference. Even as I write this it seems too late to change anything. You probably already know how this will end, or at least you think you do. That's because you've been watching the news. I just want to record for posterity the small role I played in this monstrous, monstrous chain of events. Whether I acted hastily or refused to act at all, whether I came off like a shrill, hysterical little asshole (as I occasionally—erroneously do) or whether I am actually seen in the proper light amid all the incredible events of the past few months, especially considering the personal problems I was having at the time, whether I can put all this across or not … the important thing is that I did the best I could. I'm sure you would have done better.

My parents, my friends, everyone I have ever known have said to me, at one time or another, "You shouldn't be allowed to keep pets." Dorothy, my unlamented ex-girlfriend, who used to live here with her late, unlamented cat, Mrs. Brisbee, told me I shouldn't be allowed near animals of any kind. She claimed that fish could take just one look at me and die, and that even though they were allegedly my fish, she was always the one who had to feed them.

"Oh, yeah, Dorothy, that must be why they starved to death!" For some reason, she seemed to find that remark hilarious.

The particular setup to which she was referring was, in fact, my most successful aquarium ever. It was in the old twenty-gallon. It was a community tank, and out of the original twenty fish, the last one survived for almost four months. I must have spent nearly a hundred dollars trying to keep the population up for the next year, but it seemed worth it, even with the frequent deaths and replacements.

And meanwhile, Dorothy was growing tired of me. She took to threatening to throw furniture at me. She made a crack about my virility in front of her mother, insulted my personal hygiene in front of my mother, stalked the apartment all stony faced, making noises with everything but her mouth in front of my friends, itemized everything she'd ever bought for me and all the money I owed her over the eight years we went out, and then, after all that, gave me the boldest slap of all.

She asked me to marry her. And she made a big scene of it, explaining how everything she had done had only been a distress signal, and that this was our last big chance together …

It would be pointless and painful to detail the complex series of events that followed her proposal. I don't clearly understand them myself, but I'm sure some of them were my fault. Say, thirty percent. But two months after her so-called proposal she moved out, took half of the furniture, half of my record collection, books, tools, dishware. All she really left me was Mrs. Brisbee. Which, in light of everything else, should give you a pretty good idea of how much Dorothy thought of Mrs. Brisbee.

But forget all that. The important point is that while all this was going on, all the fish died.

Which is to say, I stopped buying them. There no longer seemed to be a point. The water looked as though it could kill a fish instantly.

On the day Dorothy moved out, I asked her how she'd

like me to hold her head under that water and she told me she thought it would taste better than a goodbye kiss from me. So I asked her if she thought it was so important for peoples' kisses to taste good and wondered aloud how ancient couples resolved problems like mouth and body odors and whether they'd broken up on account of them.

"I think not!" I declared, slipping in front of her to block the door.

Eventually she got out. Her final insult was, believe it or not, a remark about the aquarium.

Once she got out I fell into another of my depressions, thinking of the eight years I'd wasted trying to cultivate and refine that bitch. Then I ... acted out.

Which might have worked out all right, except that I momentarily forgot that even a paperback book—if thick enough—if thrown hard enough—and at the proper angle, can break the glass on a twenty-gallon aquarium.

So, in spite, or because of everything, I cleaned up the aquarium. With a carpet shampooer. It was during this debacle that Mrs. Brisbee, watching me from atop a speaker cabinet, realized at last just how much she hated me. She just sat there while I cursed and fumed and beyond all else—got the job done—and she stared at me with her eyes half-shut in contempt. I wished I had something to feed her to.

Kitty litter, like most things, only more so, becomes more economical when bought in greater quantities. So I buy fifty-pound bags at the pet store. It was there, while trying to haggle for a discount on two fifty-pound bags, that I saw the aquarium sale.

It had only been two weeks since that day ... and already I yearned to set up a whole new aquarium. And there, directly before me, was my ideal tank, a fifty-five-gallon aquarium, hood, light wood grain stand and filter, all for only a hundred and eighty-nine bucks.

Maybe it was a stupid idea, but at the time it seemed like an inspiration. I acted so impulsively and it seemed to take so damn long to find any reason to regret it, that I just reveled in the experience. It brought me back to life and had the immediate effect of getting me the much haggled discount on my hundred pounds of kitty litter.

I spent more money landscaping that aquarium than on probably all the other setups I'd ever had, and I spent almost a week setting it up, going back and forth to the pet store, selecting each rock, plant, background, with studious deliberation and care. My prize catch was a large, porous, hideously-shaped piece of black rock. There was a whole barrel full of the things. I ended up buying a second, smaller piece which I ended up not even having room for. When I asked the pet shop guy why he didn't use any of them in his store displays, he pretended he didn't know where the barrel came from, looking at it as though for the first time. Looking back on it, I realize he may not have been pretending after all ...

But anyway, I threw myself into this project with almost hysterical dedication. I should add, at this juncture, that Mrs. Brisbee actually showed considerable interest in the project. She was drawn in so wholeheartedly to the festive atmosphere that she forgot to eat for several days, which is just as well, because for those several days, I forgot to feed her.

Then came the final decision. With what should I stock my aquarium? Of course, saltwater fish were out of the question. Too much money, too much work, too many garish colors. And of course, they'd all be dead in a week. Live-bearers— swordtails, platys, black mollies, and guppies didn't warrant anything as big as a fifty-five-gallon aquarium. I didn't want another community tank for sixty-odd tetras, rasboras, danios, gouramis, barbs, and catfish.

It had to be a unique population. A single piranha would be a waste of space, and any more would have made me a nervous wreck. There are plenty of large and unconventional aquarium fish: arowana, elephant noses, knife fish, plecostomes ... But in the end, I went with cichlids, the most intelligent and dramatic of all fish. I looked at Oscars, angelfish, discus, convicts, firemouths, severums, and a half-dozen varieties of African mouthbreeders. I ended up with a dozen small Jack Dempseys, Cichlosoma biocellatum. They were no more than two inches long now, but—if they lived—they'd grow to be seven or eight inches long. They were beautiful, shimmering with scatterings of yellow and aqua blue scales, raising their dorsal crests and opening out their gills to double the apparent size of their heads as they squared off in plastic traveling bags.

It was amazing how quickly those twelve little fish filled out that fifty-five-gallon tank. They performed constantly. You could watch their faces as they swam their threatening patterns and almost feel an intelligence at work.

They seemed to double their size in the first two weeks. Their colors brightened, their dorsal fins grew long and threatening, they brawled, danced, followed my and Mrs. Brisbee's movements constantly. Far from starving them, I fed them three times a day, three different kinds of food, with live brine shrimp and tubifex worm feasts all weekend.

As my so-called friends had sold out to Dorothy, I found plenty of time to spend with my fish. I admired my landscaping, the fish, the constant flow of bubbles—all the things I'd never noticed or appreciated before. I didn't watch television, listen to music, read or take a shower. I did remember to feed Mrs. Brisbee, whose name unaccountably seemed to be turning to Dorothy. But most of the two consecutive weekends were spent staring at the growing fish, drinking beer and humming pathetically along with the almost inaudible hum of the pump.

It was on the second Sunday evening that I first noticed the reddish-brown cloud rising from the largest hole in the porous black rock.

But before I get into that, I should mention something about the fish dreams I was beginning to have around this time. During that brief period when everything in the aquarium seemed fine and healthy, I had two or three of them every night:

I'm a fish ... Dorothy's a fish ... Dorothy the cat is a fish ... I'm on a subway train and I turn into a fish, slowly, one piece of me at a time, as I look frantically for water while dust rises from every surface ... I open the bottom drawer of my dresser, and thousands of flopping, talking fish begin to gush out onto the floor ... every wall of my apartment is a gigantic aquarium and I'm imprisoned in an exitless maze of glass walls behind which huge, impossibly exotic fish talk to me and each other over a crackling intercom system.

Stuff like that.

I was beginning to grow phylum-conscious. That expression, I might add, was introduced to me by a twenty-foot scorpion fish in one of these dreams. Phylum conscious. It took me way too long to figure out what the fish meant by that.

And meanwhile, there was the cloud. It was brown and red and held what appeared to be tiny, wriggling specks. I figured the brine shrimp were trying to spawn inside the rock. So it wasn't the compact little cloud rising slowly from the hole in the rock that alerted me. It was my Jack Dempseys' reaction to the cloud. They looked frightened half to death.

Occasionally one would dart out towards the patch of brown and snap threateningly along its edges, trying to swallow up some of the tiny, wriggling creatures. But in an instant it darted away again. The fish hovered no closer than a foot but no further than fifteen inches from the hole in the rock, their eyes on it all the time. They could be distracted by food … but only momentarily.

So it was the fish that drew me to it. I had to see what they saw.

I was annoyed. I laughed at myself and thought, "Aww, Christ … HERE IT COMES!" and just about decided then and there that there was only one thing to do: go buy some tablets that would clear up the problem.

At the pet shop I talked to the guy and he told me it must just be a few brine shrimp breeding in the rock. He didn't seem to understand that I was positive they weren't brine shrimp. I barely got the chance to tell him, because he was talking about how more and more it seemed as though brine shrimp were tolerating fresh water, and what a cool thing that was. I told him that had nothing to do with me and demanded that he give me something to clear up the water. I ended up getting algaecide pills and cloudy water pills. I paid six bucks for it and knew all along it wouldn't work.

"You know, maybe you just didn't clean out the rock very well. Sometimes you gotta soak 'em for a while, you know?"

I had one in my hand now, standing over the barrel. There didn't seem to be as many of them now. This one was about half the size of mine but still had the same twisted black angles, shot full of yawning holes. I noticed an aquarium display, minus the water, at the front of the store.

"Hey, what the hell are you doin'?"

"This is one of them."

"This is what?"

"Like the rock in my tank. The one that's clouding."

"Damn. This is one might fine looking rock here. Ugly as shit ... but cool."

Things didn't improve. Within a week it spread throughout the water. I took the rock out of the tank and washed it under hot water for ten minutes, but it didn't even discolor the water.

And the fish ... well, they were pale and they always seemed to be curled up in the corner, or hiding in the plastic plants. They barely ate. And they stayed as far away from the rock as possible. So I took it out again. I washed it. I examined it. And then noticed that the rock made no difference. The fish still cowered as far from the source as possible, but now the source could move. They would slink along the glass or dart from plant to plant, all as a unit, and cluster again in a different corner. I would wait for such an occasion and watch them, watch their eyes, trying to see the movement of whatever was frightening them away. I couldn't see anything.

And so the rock went back in.

And then there were eleven. It was easy to count them. They never moved anymore except as a group. I counted and re-counted them, but there was no point in it. There were only eleven fish. And no trace of the twelfth.

So, they were cannibals. I thought, good! Let them eat each other! I could use a good laugh! But then I looked at them, yellowing, curling their heads towards their tail fins, all fins flattened against the body and undulating in quick, weak strokes.

No ... maybe it just ... jumped out ... and DOROTHY GOT IT! Dorothy the cat, I mean.

You may be asking yourself what is the point in elaborating

on all this insignificant detail. Get on with it, you say. But you see, it's the apparent insignificance that you have to understand! You have to see how it was, and understand, and say, "Naah, I wouldn't have done anything, either."

The second fish died a week after the first, the third died five days after that, and the fourth died four days after that. Each time I'd fumble through the aquarium with my hands, with a net, searching for the corpse. And then I'd kick Dorothy the cat in case she had something to do with it.

By the time the fifth fish had disappeared the water was so cloudy I really couldn't trust my eyes, and so based my suspicion on the fact that a fish was by now scheduled to disappear, and that if I therefore couldn't see it, it was missing. I could see the other pale and bent Jack Dempseys drifting listlessly on one side of the aquarium, gradually becoming lost in the brown cloud that wriggled with tiny life.

After that, I gave up. I didn't bother to feed them, didn't bother to turn on the hood light. For about a week I couldn't bring myself to even look in the aquarium. And yet, it was such a big thing, that it was considerable effort not to look at it.

And meanwhile, there was the rest of my life, which, believe it or not, still seemed a bit more important at the time. There were my so-called friends, of course, who had written me off, evidently, even though they continued hanging out with me three or four nights a week, if only for the extra opportunities it would give them to remind them of that fact.

The women in our little group couldn't stop talking about Dorothy, although in fact their talk never came around to anything along the lines of Dorothy and I getting back together, or, oh, what cute couple we had been, but seemed to run something along the lines of: oh, guess what what well I talked to the Dot today no kidding well how is she oh you know Dottie she's just having the time of her life oh that's so nice to hear have you seen her new place no oh god it's so nice and well you know ... so clean!

As though they were talking about someone I didn't know. I find it hard to believe that they had any reason to bring it up other than just to torture me.

The dismal state of my social life was enough to dull and obscure the frustration of fifty-five gallons of water going to hell in my living room. Somehow a week went by without my giving the aquarium so much as a single close look.

When I finally brought myself to turn on the aquarium light, I was horrified. The water was almost opaque. A single, unaccountably bloated fish hovered along the right side of the tank, its mouth moving as though it were chewing gum. It looked bigger than I'd remembered, and its stomach was plump and swollen. And then I realized why. The cloud was suffused with tiny wriggling creatures, too small to please a robust cichlid but plentiful enough to keep it alive. I strained my eyes to catch sight of another survivor, but I could see none. The lone Jack Dempsey hardly moved at all, except for an occasional lunge at the glass thermometer that stood weighted at the bottom. The thermometer would clank loudly against the side of the tank and then the fish would disappear among the rocks and plastic plants.

I could see that there was something unusual about the way this aquarium was going to seed. After all, I'd experienced this so many times, I had a pretty clear notion of all the steps and variations of the scenario. This was different. Something was in that water, clouding it continually, faster than any sediments could build up, clouding it with tiny living creatures that a fish could live on. Then what was happening to all the fish?

It seemed to be a reflection on the state my whole life was collapsing into. Somehow I felt that if my life were to take a turn, or had taken a turn back when I'd bought the aquarium, the tank wouldn't be so clouded, such a shit-laden disaster.

One night I was in a deceptively good mood and forgot about the aquarium entirely, caught up in the revelry of a minor coup I masterminded at work (which I won't go into now), when out of nowhere, Dorothy called me. It was the first time we'd talked in about a month. She sounded pleasant enough as she asked me if she could come over and pick up a few things and visit with Dorothy (Mrs. Brisbee), so I suddenly poured out all my good cheer at her, inviting her over and promising to break open some wine for the occasion.

It's almost too humiliating to describe the elaborate steps I took to prepare for the visit, which I'd expected and had been dreading ever since she'd walked out on me. I was like a little girl getting ready for the first day of school—changing my clothes, brushing my hair in every imaginable direction, trying to figure out which one gave the best illusion that I had a reasonably full head of hair. I had put on some cologne that she had bought for me four years ago that I had never used. I made the bed. I got out a bottle of wine—actually, three bottles, the remaining contents of which just about added up to a full bottle. So I made three into one. I brought out all of her favorite albums, which I'd hidden when she moved out. I even cleaned the place—washed the dishes and polished the tabletops and cleaned the catbox and practiced calling the cat Mrs. Brisbee.

I took one last tour of the living room. Without looking—without even thinking about it—I clicked on the aquarium light. I don't really know now—was I just seeing it through Dorothy's eyes, seeing for the first time just how far gone the aquarium was, or had it gotten that much worse in the last few days? A dead, opaque brown. The only thing visible in it was a fuzzy fish head floating along the front glass. Somewhere along the line, the filter had broken down.

I lifted the lid. The stench was horrendous. As I jerked away I suddenly realized the whole place smelled of it. It would be the first thing Dorothy noticed when she walked in the door. I panicked. I turned off the light. I threw a sheet over it. I might as well have spotlit it. I could just hear the cracks, the lecture, the smug satisfaction as she shook her head at it.

I won't try to articulate the flurry of thoughts that collided at that moment. My stomach fell away and I felt what I was sure—what I was hoping—was that telltale crushing pain in my chest that meant I'd be dead and happy about it by the time she walked in.

And the doorbell rang.

I screamed. It felt good—about as good as anything was going to feel for a long time. So I screamed again. And the doorbell rang again. And again.

So I swallowed hard, gave up on all the hopeless fantasies

that I'd been brewing for the past hour, all of which, I see now, would have gone wrong anyway. I went to the door, trying to think of a way to get her in and out of the apartment quickly without her seeing the aquarium.

By the time I opened the door, I must have looked like I was in a seething rage, because when she saw me the dainty little smile she'd been wearing fell away, her eyes bulged in shock and she backed away. I looked her over. She had on a cute little blazer, a nice tight tee shirt and form-accentuating jeans. Her hair was cut in a new way that flattered her already—okay, I admit it—quite pretty face. I don't know what she had in mind when she came over to see me, but I'd like to think I could make a pretty accurate guess. That, coupled with all the little fantasies I'd been rehearsing myself, made my next move even more painful. But there was nothing in the world—sex, the hope of reconciliation—that was worth her reaction to the aquarium, the reaction I could recite without ever having heard it—which isn't quite true because I'd heard it a thousand times already. Hadn't I? Of course I had.

"What's the matter? Flush your keys down the toilet?"

Her voice was weak and shaken. "I—I thought it'd be a good idea to ring. I mean, I haven't been here in a month."

"A whole month? Well, well, no kidding. I can't imagine what you could have left here that could all of a sudden be so important after a whole month."

I have to admit I almost faltered here. She looked utterly crushed.

"Are you all right? I ... I ..." She sniffed. "Oh, god, that smell."

"Aww, come on! Is that it? You came over to find out if I've taken a bath recently? I'm really sorry. I showered just a half hour ago ... just for you. Evidently my stench is indelible. Well, I'm really sorry about that. So fucking sorry."

And then the tears. Not falling, just collecting, waiting for the signal to gush down her artfully blushed cheeks. "Aren't you going to let me in?"

I was weakening. I was acting out in ways she'd seen so many times, making an ass out of myself just to drive her away even though I didn't want her to go away at all. It was the momentum carrying me, as it had always been, once the momentum of unhinged temper, now the momentum of shame and embarrassment. So when the tears rolled, I just laughed.

"I don't think so, Dorothy. Why don't you just tell me what the hell it is you want and I'll bring it out, or bring it over. But don't do me any fucking favors."

"I thought ..." she shook her head and forced out a laugh. "You bastard! I thought somehow we were ... on the phone you sounded so ..."

She shrugged and looked at me cold, the color in her face gone, her mouth set as I remembered it best, grinding and ready to unleash a cargo of venom.

"Thanks for reminding me what a jerk you really are. I'm amazed I could have forgotten so quickly. You know damn well that I came over here ... oohh, you BASTARD!"

She turned away and began to storm down the hallway, turning back just long enough to scream, "And you'd better fumigate your fucking apartment before you get the whole damn building condemned."

I know that's what she said because I could still hear her even though I slammed the door on the word "fumigate."

I collapsed against the door and slid down to the floor, where I must have sat for the next two hours. Had I been a real man, I probably would have cried. As it was, I just whimpered and whined and complained to myself, trying to squeeze out a few tears. It felt like I was masturbating.

That night I awoke, for the first time, to a noise that was to cost me a lot of sleep in the days to come. It was so loud, so sharp, that the first time I heard it I was sure someone had just broken into the apartment. I crept from the bed and stood in the bedroom doorway, listening for it to repeat. When it did, and I pinpointed its source, I felt the horror for the first time.

Something was in the aquarium, furiously attacking the thermometer, banging it into the glass. I could hear the water churn, I could hear the gravel stirring as though something that was too big to be a Jack Dempsey were thrashing back and forth across the bottom of the tank. I did not turn on the light.

In fact, I didn't turn on the aquarium light for quite a while. It's not that I wasn't curious, it's just that my fear overrode any curiosity that lurked underneath. Not only was I afraid ... I had to deny to myself that I was afraid. I told myself every night that I would step through the door to find only a dead, brown-clouded fish tank that was smelling the place up and was just going to have to be emptied, washed, and probably put on end at the back of a deep closet.

But what I'd find instead was the fury, hidden in the churning opaque fluid, splashing through the hood and dripping like splattered blood down the wall. I wouldn't stand any closer than three feet from it, and always averted my eyes when it began to stir. I tried to pretend it wasn't happening, even as I spent every instant I was in that living room ... aware of it ... listening to it ... waiting.

Maybe it had something to do with that ugly scene with Dorothy. That was, after all, what I'd spent the whole day thinking about. Instead of wondering what kind of creature it could be, who to call in, how to kill it myself ... and how this could possibly be happening, I'd spend all day regretting what a fool I'd made of myself in front of her, or smirking to myself about how well I managed to scare off the clinging wench, or conjuring up ever more unlikely reconciliation dramas or dreaming up clever little put-downs with which I'd lace my final—evidently quite lengthy—kiss-off speech, or just staring at her pictures, which still filled my desk drawers.

I knew it was ... well, if not important, at least ... unique.

But it just didn't seem to trap my attention unless I was in the same room with it, at which point it paralyzed me, drove me out at night, kept me awake when I was too exhausted to leave the apartment. But I couldn't focus on it.

This lasted an entire week. I came out of it gradually; trying slowly to get a grip on myself, steel myself for the truth in that murky water. I noticed the cat ... whatever her name was ... ready to spring at something that frightened it. She'd stare at it and I'd try to avoid seeing it by looking at her. But she wouldn't break her stare, and sooner or later, I'd end up turning my own eyes aquariumward.

It didn't take long to spot an occasional long flap of pink flesh brush against the glass, the barbed white strips that would appear suddenly against the glass and peel away like tentacles.

It was almost impossible to get a stable impression of what it looked like or even how big it might be. Every little glimpse offered another incongruous detail, another hint that seemed to contradict every other hint.

Braced by the cat's fascination, I began to watch it. I learned that it did no good to turn on the aquarium light. When I did, the water would stop splashing, the thermometer would stop clattering against the glass. It seemed to shrink out of existence. But once the top light was shut off, it would stir up again … staining the walls, and eventually creaking at the wooden stand which no longer seemed as strong as it once had.

The cat eventually got up the courage to jump onto the aquarium hood, and stand there petrified, as an occasional tendril or horn or claw leapt from the water and banged on the lid or the light casing.

It was obvious from the start that it knew when the cat was up there. Its attacks against the hood got so aggressive that it seemed only a matter of time before it jumped out of the tank entirely.

But then, within a few days, its attacks toned down, and became intermittent tappings. It was taunting the cat, trying to lure it into the tank. It didn't take much to see her, confident enough to lie down on the aquarium lid, as totally outmatched by the shape-changer in the water.

Life had never offered Mrs. Brisbee much. She was strictly a house cat, an only cat, a heavy, listless cat who had never had much fun in her life. Neither Dorothy nor I ever played with her, and she'd long since ceased to expect it. Life was sleeping and eating. And the food was dry. It was all she could really hold down. I guess the attraction of something that worked constantly to get and keep her attention was just too much to resist.

She was scared. Even as she trusted it enough to fall asleep on top of the aquarium, there were times when its banging would awaken her and she would arch and shiver as, underneath the hood, incredibly fast appendages—claws on jointed arms, or tentacles or tongue or all of these and more, jabbed out of the water's surface to bounce the cat along the top of the hood.

In her last few days, she had to be lifted off the hood and planted in front of her food. Within minutes, she would be back atop the aquarium, ready to sleep or cower, whichever the thing inside preferred.

On the night it happened, I went drinking with three of the people I worked with and came in feeling a bit cranky about not having told off all three of them over a few rotten turns each had done me in the past few months, at having gone out of my way to be engaging and funny and pleasant and not coming off any better than I would have had I just told them all off and stormed out. All this seemed terribly important when I came through the door, mainly because it was the easiest thing to think about in my drunken state ...

Because I was very drunk. Drunk enough to stand in transfixed horror before the creaking, swaying aquarium stand and the fury just barely concealed in the thick brown soup, and not be able to move even as I realized that ... somehow ... it was stronger and more vicious and determined than ever before. I could catch the glints of light on the appendages that darted out from the water and banged the lid, sending the frenzied cat into hysterics as she bounced awkwardly atop the rattling hood. Why didn't she jump off?

Why didn't I grab her and lock her in the bedroom with me? I was drunk enough, and sick and dizzy enough to lose sight of all that as I came out of my trance, stumbled into my room and collapsed, still wearing my coat and shoes, atop my semi-made bed. Something was about to happen. I could see that clearly. And yet I was too far gone to care. I was asleep instantly and would have stayed that way for another twelve hours ...

I don't know if it was a noise that woke me up. The first thing I noticed was the silence, as though that silence was fresh and abrupt enough to awaken me. As I believe it did. I stood and crept through the darkness toward the aquarium.

By the streetlight I could see that the hood had fallen off entirely. The aquarium was still and silent. I lifted the hood from the floor and began calling to the cat as I refitted the hood and clicked on the light.

I called out to the cat for the next couple of days. The more foolish I felt, the more I was compelled to call out to her, and the more oppressive became the silence that followed. I envisioned a struggle between the two of them, Mrs. Brisbee dragging it across the floor in their death struggle, and both of them now dead and decomposing under the furniture somewhere.

I was convinced that this was what had happened. I was sure the aquarium was now empty.

And yet, I didn't drain it and clean it. I almost did, but then lost my nerve.

On the day the fury came back to life, I found a chewed, rounded piece of bone lying wet and slimy on the living room floor.

Mercifully, it came back slowly, as if out of a long sleep.

The first thing I noticed was the ridge, about an eighth of an inch high and anywhere from two to ten inches long, swimming across the water's surface. I noticed that the water level was dropping almost to the halfway point, so I dechlorinated about ten gallons of water and dumped it all in before I went to bed.

Which might have been my biggest mistake.

That fresh water did something that neither I nor the creature in the aquarium wanted. The water began to clear.

Before I even saw the aquarium the next morning, I could hear it moaning and crying.

The water was a translucent grey except for the thick brown ooze settling over the gravel, the rocks and the shapeless, motionless creature slumbering noisily there. I could barely bring myself to look at it ... it seemed so big, almost like a dog.

And of course you ask how I could continue to harbor this monstrosity. I can't write these words without wondering myself. Oh, things have changed a great deal since then, of course, and sometimes I wonder just what I thought was going on during this transitional phase. No matter how I try, I always end up trying to justify my actions according to what I was thinking at the time, though I doubt seriously I was doing any thinking at all.

Oh, it was horrible—what I could see of it, mottled, bulbous mounds riddled with veins, horn-like protuberances, the twisted and entwined appendages tucked beneath it and a thick cord running from its center cavity up to the water's surface, where it blossomed into half a dozen lotus-like outcroppings. It looked as though it could weigh at least forty pounds.

And it was dying in my living room.

Suddenly I was struck with purpose. I didn't weigh the situation. I never stopped to ask why. I just realized that, somehow, I couldn't let it die. It was just too … I just couldn't let it happen.

At first I thought I'd just feed it ground beef. But a strange feeling came over me as I stood there watching the beef defrost in the microwave oven. I could hear its pathetic moaning even over the hum of the microwave, and I realized, as I watched that plate of raw meat go around and around, that this tasteless, boneless, hairless hunk of beef would never satisfy it. It just wasn't good enough. I could live on it—I could make thousands of dishes with it, but none of these would satisfy or even stir the thing in the aquarium.

So I went back to the pet shop.

I deliberated quite a bit about what kind of animal to feed it. I started off with grisly and otherwise impractical notions: birds, dogs … I thought of cats … but no. I felt truly awful about what I'd let happen to Mrs. Brisbee. Obviously it was my fault that she was dead. I could see that then just as I see it now. And I did feel guilty about it, guilty enough not to be able to even look into the pen of kittens at the store. But at the time I was so consumed by the importance of keeping it fed that I took the cat's death as a justifiable, even noble sacrifice.

I determined to bring him home the finest living meal my stomach could stand the thought of.

I checked out lizards, turtles, and snakes. I mean, I like reptiles, and still, in my heart, believe that reptiles are the ultimate pets and … in terms of my own experience, the most rewarding companions. But every iguana, turtle or garter snake in the place looked as though it would be a severe letdown after a plump meal like Dorothy. Mrs. Brisbee, that is.

I settled for two obvious and inexpensive and—as it turned out—fortuitous choices: ten goldfish and two white rats.

The pet shop guy was the same one I'd been dealing with every month for the last five years, and yet he didn't seem to recognize me at first. Me or anything else. He was slow, distracted, disturbed. He mumbled under his breath.

Suddenly, his female coworker came running and crying out of the back room.

"It died, Charlie. It just fell … apart," collapsing into a sobbing fit right in front of us. Charlie tried to calm her down, walking her back towards the rear of the store, whispering to her, but when he stepped back behind the counter I could see that he was just a hair's edge more composed than she, and was fighting back tears as he looked at me and smiled.

"Sorry, sir, one of our …" His expression changed, his mouth and eyes widening. "It's you."

"Me? Yeah, what about me?"

"I mean, I'm sorry, sir. It's just … you are the gentleman who bought that fifty-five-gallon tank and that black rock, and was … um, having problems with your water clouding up?"

"Yeah, that's me."

He smiled and then looked over the countertop, his face flushing, looking at the selection he'd helped me pick out and package, as though seeing it for the first time.

"Omigod," his voice screeched up an octave. "What are you going to do with all these animals?"

"I'm going to skin them and make clothes out of them."

"I'm sorry. Ha! Ha! Ha! I don't know what came over me, sir!"

He shook his head, moaned, and tried to smile. "Bad day, bad day."

I lifted my packages off the counter and was almost out the door when I realized that I'd been there for half an hour without going down the long, picturesque aisle of tropical fish, the unworthy goldfish being far off to the side of them. I decided to take a stroll up and down the aisle before leaving.

And as I did, an indescribable, inexcusable mixture of

horror and joy came over me.

I could read the signs. The rocks, the porous, thorny rocks, some in clear, heavily populated tanks, others in tanks that were in various stages of clouding, the occupants crowded and huddling on one side of the tank—always the side farthest from the rock. Some were empty, some were no more than empty spaces where there used to be tanks. The whole fish department was going to hell. And no one seemed worried about it. Not when they had a dying … dead thing in the back of the store.

It was silent and unmoving when I entered my living room with its groceries. The water was beginning to cloud a rich reddish-brown again, which I took as a good sign.

I believe that when I killed the colony off with fresh water, I was cutting off its final food supply. Even now, I could see it shrunken and shapeless. For a moment, I was sure it was dead.

I didn't see the goldfish die. They just disappeared, one by one, over the course of the evening.

Within a day, the water reached its rust-colored opacity again and within a day after that, I could actually hear activity in the tank again, even an occasional smack of glass on glass as it swatted the thermometer against what seemed to be all four sides of the tank.

So I hung on to the white rats, not because I had a problem feeding them to such a hideous creature, but because I was concerned about the ideal time to give it another big feeding. After all, I didn't want to spoil him.

And in the meantime, I began talking to him. I called him Robert. Don't ask me why I gave him my own name. It began as an occasional comment. But as the days passed, I talked to him more and more, in an increasingly confidential— no, confessional—way. I'd ask him questions. Big, important questions. And when I finally fed him the white rats, it was with the firm conviction that he hadn't really wanted or needed them until now. Just as I was convinced that he knew all about the rats because I'd told him about them.

I took a drive out to another pet shop—where I wasn't known—for my next run. I got a dozen goldfish and a half a dozen white mice. When I finally returned to the neighborhood shop, the whole fish section was closed off for renovation and remodeling. Strangely enough, they had more mammals than ever. Today there was a run on rabbits. I bought two, and three customers in front of me at the counter all had them, too.

Charlie, the guy behind the counter, was a changed man, cheerful and wise-cracking as he got us all our rabbits (no questions asked) and took our money. I felt like asking him about the … thing or things in the back of the store, but I didn't have a chance to. He just talked on and on about how popular these rabbits were and how we had to take good care of them, not recognizing me so much as recognizing all of us collectively.

But time was running out for me … for us. Soon, a fifty-five-gallon tank would be too small for him. Soon there would be too little water to keep him comfortable, to keep him masked from my squeamish scrutiny. I tried aging water as long as I could, but no matter how long I left it sitting out, it killed off the planktonic colony as soon as I added it to the aquarium, sending Robert into a whining frenzy.

I was missing more work. I was getting along poorly with the rest of the staff. Dorothy wouldn't answer my calls.

And he was beginning to wear away at the cabinet supporting him. When he went into a frenzy, the cabinet would sway too much, cracking way too much. Even during his somnolent periods the cabinet would creak.

Something would change—had to change. And I knew that this change would have little or nothing to do with me. I was just a helpless spectator, overly concerned and uncomfortably close to the action. I kept talking to him, but every once in a while I had the urge to really … let him die … even to kill him. But such weak moments were few, and were always followed by days of guilt and depression. I was never far from the thought of how dependent he was on me. And how soon this would change.

Then, one evening I came home to the usual dark apartment, kicked my shoes off at the door and took a loud, wet step onto the living room carpet. I gasped so loud it sounded as though

I was screaming and swallowing at the same time. I turned on a light.

The aquarium hood was overturned on the floor, but Robert was still in the aquarium. The noduled ridge that ran down his back and the padded extremities that floated at the water's surface were all visible.

"Robbie? Robbie, you nasty little thing, were you crawling around on the floor? Huh?" I scolded him gently as I replaced the light, my voice raised and distorted into what could only be described as baby talk.

He had been roaming the apartment, leaving a glutinous, watery trail. He'd been everywhere he could get without opening a door. Looking for food? It didn't seem possible that he could be hungry again already, and yet ... he was getting so big ...

I couldn't stand it. I went out to dinner. I went to the nearest K-Mart to check out guns at the sporting goods department, but I didn't buy any. Instead, I bought every hamster in the pet department—sixteen of them.

Two nights later, he woke me up.

He was often noisy and excitable enough to wake me, but he was quiet now, hovering silently over me as I lay in bed, dripping water and running his padded tentacles across my face and over my body.

I didn't dare open my eyes, though I'm sure he knew I was awake. I was sure that he was, at that very moment, about to make the great gastronomic leap from rodent to human.

I was awake for about ten minutes of this, wondering how long it had been going on, when he suddenly moved away from me, actually straightening his spindly, segmented legs and raised his body almost to the ceiling as he let out a long, shrill whistle.

I felt a light bounce against the bed and heard him land, strong and sure on the floor. I slowly turned and watched as he moved toward the door.

My first impression was that of a half-dozen creatures all riding on the back of a giant spider. He was mostly legs. There may have been as many as ten of them. Hanging and coiling and whipping amid these orderly, machine-like legs were at least as many tentacles, some thick, some in the shuddering act of turning from thick to thin, as though the tentacles themselves belonged to two or three different creatures, all slung limp into a shapeless mass.

But after those first few unfocused instants, I saw sparks begin to shoot off either side of Robert's great crest, exploding into twisted tendrils of light that at times seemed to cover his back like a great net as the body beneath this display seemed to shudder in and out of focus. And finally, as he rounded the corner of my door, I saw a flicker of red light deep within the torso.

I lay there gripping the sheets, trying to blink the picture out of my mind.

When I heard the crashing, I thought he had just knocked something over in his aimless wandering. But the noise didn't stop. It got louder, erupting finally into the breaking of glass.

I sat up screaming our name, jumped from the bed and ran into the kitchen. He had smashed through the window above the sink, leaving crushed pans and shattered glass in his wake.

And so now he was out. Free. I'd done nothing—hadn't called the zoo, the University, hadn't killed him, hadn't taken the damned rock back to the pet shop demanding a refund. And now it was much more than just my problem.

I didn't go to work the next day. I sat around drinking Cokes, smoking cigars, pacing the apartment, wandering the neighborhood, combing the newspapers and watching the TV newscasts, waiting for the grisly crime to surface, the crime that only I could explain.

Suddenly, what happened on the news had something to do with me.

It was already dark out before I put anything better than cut grocery bags over the kitchen window.

It was two days before he returned, two very long, agonizing and yes, very lonely days, during which nothing happened—with the exception of one or two brief, vague news stories which may have ... might have ... and as I would learn soon enough, must have had something to do with Robert.

He returned in the middle of the night, neatly popping off the plywood window patch and following the path I'd cleared for him. I heard him plopping into the cramped, unstable confines of the aquarium, groaning and sizzling as he tried to sink beneath the surface.

"Hello, Robert."

I heard a knocking and groaning from inside the tank. The particle-board beneath it creaked out a warning.

The next morning I stood over him smiling and talking as I did my tie. Two little, slime-coated translucent lumps sat above the surface, and I let myself think they were eyes.

I had the TV on in the background and managed to hear the tail end of a news story that seemed to deal with my own neighborhood. I didn't really catch much of it, but I didn't worry. The reporter's face and voice seemed too cheerful for it to have had anything to do with me.

I had to spend more money on his food. I had to buy a bigger tank, at least a hundred-gallon. I had to find a way to keep him from leaving again. I just couldn't go on this way, worrying about what I might have to hold myself accountable for ...

I'd have to work more hours. Robert was going to cost more and more as time went on, and I had to keep thinking of his feeding as an over-the-counter, pay-as-I-go, strictly legal, moral, and ethical affair.

That night I drove from work directly to the pet shop. I planned on buying every hamster, rabbit, rat, mouse and gerbil in the place. Who knows? Maybe even a few cats as well. I was just oozing good will.

What I found at the pet shop jarred my little fantasy. The big windows on either side of the door were blown away, the door was gone, the interior was gutted and the whole place blocked off by the police.

I joined a group of three people who were talking to one of the cops. He looked half bored to death as he stood there leaning to one side with crossed arms, listening to these three people, all of whom seemed on the verge of hysteria.

"Sorry, sir, the shop's closed. Ha! Closed for the duration, you might say. Ha! Ha!"

"What the hell happened?"

"No one knows, sir."

The woman next to me burst in: "This and three other shops in the area."

"Four others," piped in an old man.

"Totally ruined. Everything gone ..."

"Everything!" I was beginning to feel a little bit hysterical myself. "Omigod! Shit!" It must have been a little loud and I must have looked a bit wired, because everyone jumped or at least flinched and a cop thirty feet away turned and looked at me.

"Hey, fella," the cop intoned. "Settle down, will you?" he looked at all four of us and shook his head in disgust. "I don't know what's got into you folks."

"Listen, pal," I snarled, pushing my way through the group and standing face to face with the cop, "I need rodents, and I need 'em fast!"

He laughed. He stopped and thought about it. He laughed louder and harder and longer and turned away from us completely.

"Hey, Stuart! Ha! Ha! Get a load of this group over here!"

The three civilians on the scene didn't seem to think it funny at all. They were withering, withdrawing into their own dread, muttering to themselves. I could only make out one audible phrase, and I couldn't even tell who said it: "What am I going to do?"

We all nodded sadly.

All the way home, my head swam. The things, breaking out and destroying the shop. Those three people. And the cop, laughing not so much at me, but all of us as a group.

And god. Oh, God, God. Me walking in the door. I can barely stand to think of it now, let alone pass it on in print. He was gone, of course. The apartment didn't look so bad, considering.

The slime trail was much more purposeful this time. There was no more than ten inches of water in the aquarium. And there was ... there was ...

I do feel responsible. I do. But not this responsible.

There was a slimy mess on the floor, a regurgitation, as it turned out.

I didn't mean to examine it. I picked it up with about forty wadded up paper towels and noticed immediately beneath the soft, flowing slime was something hard. Something long and thin.

It flopped back onto the floor as I tried to lift the mass into the garbage can.

It was an arm.

I turned away, screaming, and let out three dry retches. It was an arm, a human arm, and it … it … was … It wasn't very big.

He hasn't come back. At first I thought he would. I left the arm—wrapped, of course in the refrigerator for an entire day, thinking he would return to me, hungry, remembering the little morsel he'd left behind.

And then things started happening that made me realize that he probably wouldn't be coming back at all. It was on the evening news. A string of grisly the reporter actually used the word monstrous—crimes in this and two neighboring towns stirred recognition in me.

There is way too much food out there, too much room, too much darkness, and too much water running beneath our streets. He's never coming back.

For awhile I was sure there was a chance. I began to call Dorothy, trying to reconcile with her, trying to show how much I've changed, explaining why I'd behaved so foolishly for all those years, telling her how beautiful she'd looked that last time I saw her and how good and kind and patient she'd been with me all those years and all the while thinking about what a great meal she would be for Robert.

Ultimately, it didn't work out. It couldn't have worked out. I see this now, now that it's all over and I can reflect on my abominable behavior. Things are going to be different now. I'm putting in more time at work. I'm bathing more. I'm socializing more. I catch myself falling into the same old traps, but I fight the urge to make abusive, astringent comments about subjects of which I know nothing. I find I have less to say because of it, but that's all right, too. There will be other things to say. I'll think of something.

And the murders continue. People are, quite simply, being eaten, their scraps scattered in bouquets of blood. The news folks have had a great time with all this, always wondering just how much gore they can get away with showing—especially now, during Sweeps Week. I recognize Robert's handiwork, his and his kindred. I know I should feel worse than I do. I'm working at feeling bad about all this carnage, trying hard to fight this feeling of … pride. I should be afraid. Everyone is afraid. But not me. I'm marked. I'm a friend.

And then there are the fish dreams. They've come back. Last night the twenty-foot scorpion fish in the aquarium-labyrinth called me a traitor to my phylum. Which, of course, I am. That and … much worse. But I'm working on it.

And I think of all those people buying rabbits that day. And that other day little more than a week later, with those three people talking to the cop in front of the trashed storefront. If only we could have acknowledged our link, our kinship. Ex-changed phone numbers …

The store is no more. And Robert is gone. And there's no way to replace him …

Wait a second! Where did I …

Yes, that's it! There was a second rock, a smaller one I didn't use. Where the hell is it? Where would I put it? In the closet with my aquarium maintenance supplies? In a dresser drawer? In any kind of drawer? In the pantry? In a closet?

In the cabinet under the sink!

Oh, yes, oh god, here it is! No, no, it isn't so small at all, is it? And here, deep in this central hole, the light crackle of something dry and soft, a chrysalis deep within the rock and the tiny form within, barely noticeable beneath my fingertips.

Yes … it won't take more than two or three days to re-landscape the aquarium, restock it, overload it with fish, cheap fish, fat and worthless fish—chordata be damned!—and then … and then … little fella, you'll hatch, you'll infuse the water with your wriggling rust-colored friends and I swear to whatever god will still have me that I'll feed you anything you want, I'll feed you Dorothy and every dog and cat and worthless derelict I can find …

Just don't leave me little fella, I can love you and feed you and talk to you and teach you to talk to me and let you live in my bathtub or whatever it takes to hold you because I've had it with the human race and anything even remotely related to it. I can grow you from almost nothing, a soft, dry, crinkled patch inside a rock, into a magnificent animal! You'll thrive. You can survive—flourish because of everything within me that's killed or driven away anything or anyone that's ever come close to me, you see? You need me because of what I am that all those poor fools out there—oh, I'll bring them to you soon enough—could never be. I'm a meager, vicious animal, little fella, I'm nothing, a coward, but I'll be brave for you, little fella, for your love, for your fidelity, little fella, so that you'll never leave me, little fella, so I'll love you, little fella …

And you'll be mine.

THE SHABBIE PEOPLE

I

Their skin was smooth and colorless, so translucent that it looked like a liquid held in place by a thin glutinous membrane. The long, loose threads along the edges of their shapeless garments seemed to wave in synchronized patterns, like cilia or some delicate reef-dwelling invertebrate. Even now I believe the Shabbies were human beings, although it seems that as time goes on that I base this conviction more and more on a desperate hope that has less to do with them—or even her—than it does with the way I cling to the notion of my own humanity.

I had a job in those days. Five days a week I rode the "L" train downtown, where I immediately took a narrow set of stairs down to Lower Wacker Drive, a bleak, dust-blanketed stretch of road that ran directly beneath Wacker Drive proper and alongside the Chicago River. It was not a short cut—in fact, it added a good five minutes to my walk—and the only excuse I had for preferring it to a shorter, street level route was that it was cooler in summer and warmer (because of the heating vents from the buildings) in winter. But I walked Lower Wacker for the darkness, for the solitude. At street level I would have been no better than the rest of the office workers and clerks: in a hurry to get to work or to their trains, all milling and colliding and seething beneath the screeching elevated trains.

On Lower Wacker I'd see transients scattered along the catwalk, many asleep between scraps of newspaper and cardboard in the early morning. Otherwise there were only those few commuters who parked their cars in the designated spaces between the catwalk and the street itself. Occasionally a car would slow and the driver—hoping to claim a parking space—would ask if I was going to my car. I would cast the driver an accusing, condescending glare and simply say, "I don't drive."

I would look up at the concrete ceiling and listen for the sounds of heavier traffic flowing above, but I never heard it. Sometimes that ceiling seemed to be a mile or more thick, and the blackest, sootiest patches on it the entrances to vast, inaccessible caves.

On the morning I first encountered them I was going down the steps when I saw a haggard old man with worried eyes waiting for me at the foot of the stairs. Before I even made it to the bottom he was talking to me. I averted my eyes and attempted to pass him by, but he held out a shaking hand to block my path.

It was then that he said the word, not as part of a sentence, but just as a single, exhausted exclamation: "Shabbie."

As I attempted to sidestep him, I lost my balance and nearly fell onto the dusty, glass and ratshit-laden sidewalk. I cursed the old man and continued on my way.

I knew what he'd been talking about as soon as I saw them. There were about twenty on that first day: men and women—none of them standing any closer than ten feet from each other—on the catwalk, among the parked cars at the foot of the catwalk, even along the edges of the road. They didn't look at anything except each other, with vacant, expressionless faces, hands deep in their pockets, hugging shapeless garments around themselves. There were a few more street people hovering along the edge of this strange, scattered group. They whispered to each other, laughed, complained, but refused to pass beyond a certain point, into that arena where the brown-ragged strangers stood so silently, so oblivious to anything but each other.

Another old man called to me as I walked past the huddled transients and onto that stretch of blacktop where the strangers stood. Almost immediately I could hear a ringing, feel the pressure of an invisible fluid closing around me. I looked into their incredible eyes. If they knew I was walking among them, they made no sign; and when I finally passed the last of them I felt a tremendous release in pressure, as though I'd just surfaced from a deep dive into a swimming pool.

All the rest of that day I felt as though there was a wet gloss clinging to me, but whenever I ran my fingers over my skin, they came away dry and clean.

I didn't see them again for several days, but in the meantime I saw a piece of graffiti on one of the cement pillars that lined Lower Wacker:

"BEWARE OF THE SHABBIE PEOPLE"

It was an unseasonably cold evening in early October. For some reason I can no longer remember and probably couldn't have pinpointed at the time, my usual depression had been boiling into a vicious rage against everyone around me, against inanimate objects that got in my way, against my pathetic little room and, of course, against myself and everything about me: my thick, hopeless face, my job, my loneliness. I pushed my way through the Wabash Avenue crowds and made for the nearest stairway down to Lower Wacker Drive.

An obese rat waddled across my path. I had to stop in my tracks to keep from kicking the beast. I suddenly focused all my rage on this foul creature that had the audacity to block my way for even a split second. My fist clenched and I searched the shadows, wishing I had kicked it.

When I first heard her voice, I could swear she was laughing. It was only when I heard the telltale impact of flesh smacking flesh that I was sure she was crying—no, screaming. Then I heard the man's voice: loud, cruel, wet with lustful anger, and I realized what was going on.

They were on the catwalk, near a stairway that led to street level. I jumped onto the walk and grabbed the man before I had any idea who or what they were. With a downward straight-arm, I loosened his grip on her clothes as I grabbed his collar and swung him around to face me.

He was a Shabbie. They were both Shabbies. He was about my height, very thin, but there was an animal hunger across that emaciated face that would have scared me off had I not already been so wound up in my own furies. He screamed, a high pitched flurry of incomprehensible sounds, and his face seemed to stretch forward into a toothy snout.

I was standing too close to take a swing at him, so I brought up my elbow and struck his nose. The glancing blow stunned him long enough to allow me to step back and punch him as hard as I could with my good arm. He stumbled off the edge of the catwalk, bounced onto the hood of a car and melted into the deep shadows, moaning and whimpering.

When I turned to her she was looking at me in horror, as though I had been the sole aggressor. I opened my mouth to say something in my own defense, but she ran up the nearest set of stairs. I took one last look at the Shabbie man lying between two cars and then followed her.

She was on the top step, looking out at the city lights as though she had never seen anything like them in her life. "Are you all right? Miss? Did he hurt you?"

The sound of my voice sent a brief tremor across her face. She reluctantly turned from the skyline and looked me in the eyes.

"I didn't mean to scare you like that," I said. "Down there, I mean." Once her eyes locked into mine, she would not let go. She looked at me as though I was something disgusting she had been ordered to eat. She nodded toward the buildings, trying to draw my attention to them.

"It's a pretty skyline, isn't it?"

But she wasn't listening. I looked at her closely then, because she seemed to have lost all interest in me. Her hair was thin and medium brown, laced with sliver streaks and hanging limp and careless to her shoulders. From this vantage point, only a couple of feet away, it was almost impossible to resist trying to make out the skull beneath that clear skin and those delicate blue veins just beneath the surface. But her face was too wide— or her head was too narrow; at any rate, the effect was to jut her nose and the center of her lips forward and pull her eyes and the edges of her mouth around to the side.

I could make out her delicate slenderness even beneath the shapeless brown rags she wore. Her feet were big and her breasts were small, like a young girl's, but she was clearly more than a girl. There were traces of age and pain in her face. In spite of her plainness, her strange face and her ragged clothes, I found her unusually attractive and appealing. The fact that she was one of the Shabbie People who had been haunting Lower Wacker Drive only made the attraction stronger.

"Miss, could I … buy you something to eat? A cup of coffee or something?"

She made no response, so I turned away, humiliated, and headed for the train. I did not bother going back down to Lower Wacker; I was only two blocks from the train anyway and the crowds were beginning to thin out. As I walked I tried not to think of the capstone humiliation of this wretched day; I had saved a pretty girl from an attacker only to have my respectful advances ignored afterward. The incident seemed to have neutralized me. I no longer felt any anger, only that creeping numbness that was my biggest enemy but probably also the one thing that had kept me from taking my own useless life years before.

I went downstairs to the ticket window and showed my monthly pass. As I pushed through the turnstile I turned and saw her standing there, looking at me, looking at the turnstile and the glass booth, confused and afraid, the skin of her brows furling over her eyes.

"What?" I asked her, sounding impatient and exasperated. I was not so numb that I wasn't willing to strike out just a little at the woman who'd rebuffed me only minutes before. "What is it? Do you need money? Is that what you want? You could say something to me, you know."

I turned away and headed for the stairs, but as I reached them I heard that cry again. But this time it was not a cry of fear over a man who was beating her and probably about to rape her, but the cry of a young child, alone and lost with absolutely no idea what to do. When I turned back she was looking at the lady in the pay booth with a terrified expression.

So I did what I had to: I paid her fare. She followed me down the stairs and when the first train came and I did not get on it, she gazed thoughtfully back and forth from me to the train and then let out a sigh and relaxed at my side, no more than six inches away from me.

When my train came, we got on. There were no seats, so I had to stand, clutching a vertical bar; and when the train lurched for the first time, she grabbed the shoulder of my jacket and did not let go until we stopped at my station.

She followed me down the street, into the foyer of my building, up the steps and finally, while a quaking mixture of excitement and suspicion surged through my every limb, up to my door.

"Do you need a place to stay? Is that it?" I opened the door and she followed me in, passing by me and moving through my apartment with a timid, quiet grace, her face stretched with the same wonderment with which she'd looked at the skyline.

She was the first woman who had ever stepped into my apartment. She did not react when I shut the door and locked it, and didn't even bother to turn and look me in the face for another hour.

II

What was I to think as she moved silently through my cheap, unkempt room? She wouldn't respond to my questions, and though she seemed interested when I finally got the nerve to step into my kitchenette and fry myself a cheese sandwich, she seemed not even to understand when I offered the sandwich to her. As soon as the sizzling in the pan died, she turned away and returned to the window, where she looked out with rapt fascination upon a brick wall, a neon sign, an alley and a sliver of street.

I considered throwing her out, but of course I couldn't. This strange, but otherwise very plain young woman seemed graced by a kind of dangerous beauty when seen in the context of my lonely little apartment. I tried ignoring her as the evening progressed, drinking a beer or thumbing through a book, but I literally could not take my eyes off her, so finally I just watched her until I caught myself nodding off to sleep in my chair.

I offered her my bed, indicating with hopelessly loud and well-articulated words and awkward arm gestures that I would sleep on the couch. I lay on the couch then, a blanket pulled up to my eyes, watching her in the semi-darkness. She continued to move from one end of the apartment to the other, occasionally stopping at the window before moving on again, examining books, wall prints, the dirty plates in the sink.

The last thing I remember is her going into the bathroom and using the toilet with the door open. I could see nothing— would not even look—yet I ended up with a furious erection that followed me into sleep and writhed its way to climax in some forgotten dream.

I tried to convince her to leave the next morning. At least I told her she should. In truth, I didn't want her to leave at all. She had slept on the floor at the foot of the bed and was still there when I left. I wondered whether she would be there when I got back as I locked the bottom lock but not the top, giving her the final option—but only after debating for a full minute whether I should just lock her in.

I was thirty-four years old at the time and still a virgin. Only my hands—and even those with awkward, infrequent rendezvous—stood between me and a lifetime of abstinence. Perhaps it was because I was ugly or had difficulty speaking to people, or because of some kind of physical or social flaw to which I was simply blind. Whatever the cause, I had never slept in such close proximity to a woman, and all day I reeled with the myriad implications of that event. I fantasized that on my return home she would be communicative, thanking me for saving her virtue or maybe even her life the day before and for offering her refuge and, of course—inadvertently though it might have been—for having been a gentleman through it all.

When I returned home she was watching television. She stared at the screen as though hypnotized not by the images themselves but by the thousands of flickering signals that made up the images. I tried talking to her, I offered her food, I offered her the bed; but nothing worked. Once again she slept on the floor.

It went on this way for a week. I was growing more and more dependent on the idea that when I opened the door at night, I would find this warm, living, increasingly attractive creature placidly sharing my apartment.

Finally I gave up offering her the bed. The couch was starting to bother my back anyway, so on the seventh night I decided to sleep in the bed myself.

In a gesture of had-it-up-to-here defiance, I threw back the sheets, undressed and crawled into my bed, leaving only the hood light on in the kitchen. She stood by the refrigerator, eating pickles out of the jar and watching me with a puzzled expression. I shut my eyes as I nested in my bed for the first time in a week, sure that I'd be asleep in a minute.

I could hear her, feel her breath as she suddenly stood over me, watching me as she'd never done on the nights I'd slept on the couch. Was it our "familiarity" or was it the fact that it was such a sudden shift in routine? I was never able to figure out which of the two might have prompted her actions as I opened a single eye while she pulled the shapeless dress over her head and dropped it to the floor. The naked body underneath was sleek and had a sweet, pleasant aroma. When she pulled back the sheets and crawled in next to me, immediately folding her arms around me, I opened both eyes and gazed deep into a face that suddenly looked equally tender and eager. I leaned over to kiss her, realizing that I had never kissed a woman in my life and wasn't even close to being sure exactly how it was done.

She forced her mouth against mine in a brief, awkward struggle and after that, I just followed. My hands wandered the contours of her body in absolute disbelief while she finished undressing me. I climaxed the moment her hand glided between my legs, but she did not laugh or grow angry, and instead seemed to understand everything about me at that point. For a week she had been living on the periphery of my world, and she must have realized that beneath these sheets together we had passed beyond the edges of that world and into hers.

At least it seemed to be wholly her world. My clumsy gestures grew smoother and more acute under her guidance and as her kisses and caresses grew more passionate, I began to mimic them. My next erection followed soon after and she guided it gently into the soft, wet darkness between her thighs. We remained very still for a while after that—neither our hands nor our hips moved more than a slight quiver as she looked deep into my eyes and smiled her first real and perfect smile. By the time we began our slow rhythmic movements I knew, from the feel of our interlocked bodies and from that sweet, understanding face, that both our lives had been irrevocably changed.

When I finally slept, I dreamed of her. We were standing at the gravelly edge of a body of water at night, with only the light of a distant suspension bridge delineating us in the darkness.

She looked at me and began to speak. The things she said were shocking and horrifying, but they made perfect sense to my dream-self. I remembered the entire dream in vivid detail the next morning—all except the words she had spoken.

She grew more at ease within the grimy, chaotic confines of my apartment and widened her palate to include an increasing variety of foods in my cupboards and refrigerator. If anything, she paid less attention to me than she had before we'd first made love. As soon as I turned off the lights and crawled into bed each night, she would crawl in with me and we would make love for half the night, so that I found it almost impossible to get up in the morning for work. I finally had to start going to bed two hours earlier than usual. During sex or holding each other afterward, I seemed to be the absolute center of her life. But the next morning or the next evening, I was merely a more active, more transitory piece of furniture in a tiny room in which she seemed to be hiding from something … out there.

I gave her a name. Mona. My mother (the original Mona) died when I was four years old, and so I felt no particular attachment to the name—at least none that I realized—but it gave me comfort to bestow the name on the frail, bewildered and unceasingly curious girl. Most of the time I believed she was a simpleton and that I was doing her a favor by protecting her from the outside world, by trying to find foods she could eat, trying to teach her to speak, all the tiny gestures that seemed to fail at every turn but which, in the end, always brought her back to my bed.

I would dream of her almost every night after our lovemaking. Sometimes it would be just the two of us, sometimes there would be others, loud, shadowy and enveloped in a luminescent haze that seemed to spread for vast distances across landscapes that, as weeks progressed, became more and more uninviting, even threatening. In these dreams she was trying to lure me into the bright haze that seemed to recede from us as we approached, full of cascading, breathtaking life forms too diffuse to see clearly, but always very real and, in spite of their retreat, always very near.

III

And so Mona consumed those late fall and early winter months. We did not communicate; we rarely even looked each other in the eye and I never quite got over the sensation that she was—or would have preferred to be—completely oblivious to my presence. But I was utterly dependent on the sound of her breath, of the creaking floor beneath her feet, of the fact that this creature had consented to keep me company and in only a few months had made the vision of my past life almost unbearable to remember. And just the fact that in some strange, limited way, I was someone's lover, began to strengthen my confidence and gave me the sense that I was a functioning part of the world around me.

But she grew restless. She discovered the apartment door— as though it had never been there before. She would tug at it and pound on it and I was afraid the commotion would bring too much attention to us. So I gave her a key, taught her how to use it, bought her some winter clothes and a coat, took walks with her and, finally, because I was afraid to use the physical force to stop her, I allowed her to go out by herself. I told myself this was only right, that otherwise I was her jailer, she was my prisoner—or worse, my pet. And yet Mona was not a normal human being, was she? She was no longer with her people and I was the only thing between her and that hostile world out there, the one she had stared at with such wide-eyed amazement one night from the top of a set of concrete stairs.

Soon she began staying out late or, once in a while, all night. I couldn't ask where she'd gone, and though I considered it, I never really had the nerve to follow.

She would return with things she found on the street. I tried to keep her from bringing them in, but when I did she would suddenly grow hostile and protective. Desiccated rat and pigeon corpses, rusted shards of metal, branches, wire, all of which she would arrange methodically in the darkest corner of my apartment and hide behind a sheet. I stopped protesting, because more than disgust over the garbage she insisted on accumulating in my apartment, I felt fear of her independence. She could leave and never come back. The possibility was inconceivable.

I tried to ignore the shrine she was constructing behind the sheet. They were no longer dried corpses or discarded hubcaps and splintered boards; they were minor elements in a dense and disturbing mosaic. Mona was reconstructing something of her own world in this tiny corner of mine.

In late February I began walking to work along Lower Wacker Drive, after having avoided it completely since the day I saved Mona from her Shabbie attacker. I found no trace of them—only a cloud of white spray paint where someone had scrawled BEWARE OF THE SHABBIE PEOPLE.

I wondered where she went at night. Would she have remembered the train ride up to my neighborhood; would she know how or have money to pay and get on the "L" train and find her way down here on her own? There were times when I would linger down there as though all it would take was the right squint and the right tilt of my head in order to see them there. I wondered if she came down here to do this very thing, not knowing how to find them and trying desperately to summon them back from some inaccessible netherworld, crying out for them to take her away from this cold, bleak place and the stumpy little man who held her prisoner.

Then one night, during an unseasonably warm spell after weeks of heavy snows, I walked Lower Wacker, avoiding the widening pools and the spouts of water spilling from the streets above and whining to myself about Mona, whom I had not seen in two days. Had she disappeared for good? Could something have happened to her? I wandered Lower Wacker for a while, drinking in the desolate and expansive solitude that seemed like such a perfect extension of my mood.

The area where the Shabbies used to stand was now under a foot of water. As I stepped to the edge of this pond I saw a rat half-swim, half-scurry across it, cutting a line of splashes neatly down the middle. As the waters settled, erasing all traces of the rat's pathway, I saw what I believed to be a reflection of the ceiling above me, and my tired eyes began to unfocus along the strange contours formed there.

Suddenly there was a movement in the water, something large, struggling up from an impossible depth in this shallow pool. In the brief moment it broke the surface I was sure that it was a man, but the water settled over it and the pool grew still and silent, as though nothing had happened. I looked around; there was no one anywhere, and the green lights illuminating the underground were all flickering in synchronization.

Another splash—there it was again, exploding to the surface. Only this time it did not seem to be a man at all, but rather some kind of misshapen cephalopod, transparent and thrashing furiously before sinking once again beneath the surface. I looked carefully at the once more placid surface, then at the ceiling above. Only a reflection.

I hurried on my way, considering for a moment taking the nearest stairway up to street level and then changing my mind when I saw ominous shadows moving along the entrance to the stairway. I began to run, but there were puddles and roaring downspouts everywhere, and in the weak, still flickering green light, it was difficult to negotiate the water, and the soles of my shoes were sliding treacherously on the wet ground. Finally I stopped, leaning against a steel and concrete beam while a downpour of water roared just on the other side. I crept around to look at it more closely as I caught my breath. Was this water running down here from the street?

And then I heard it. Oh, I recognized the sound, all right. The moment I heard the voice I was sure I must be lying in bed alongside Mona and having another one of those dreams, because it was Mona herself, speaking in the voice with which she had so often called out to me in so many dreams. But it wasn't just a single woman's voice, it was several, along with manly voices that spoke in deep, threatening tones. I looked into the falling column of water and saw transparent figures struggling within, little more than water themselves, thrashing away as though trying to force their way free. I blinked and leaned closer, my face set in what must have been a ridiculous, gaping mask. I could see human forms in there, all occupying the same small spaces, trying to break away from each other. Every splash against my face felt like fingertips grasping out toward me. Finally a hand emerged, then an arm. I backed away as it reached out and then disappeared. I can't say for sure whether it sank back into the open spout of water or merely splashed shapelessly to the ground.

I screamed and ran onto the catwalk, where the shadows were heavy, but it was dry and I had quick access to the next set of stairs leading up to the street.

Though my train ride home was uneventful, I couldn't stop thinking of the hallucinations I had experienced on Lower Wacker. I arrived home in an absolute panic. Inside I found Mona, wearing one of the simple, secondhand dresses I had bought her, looking up from the television and smiling sweetly.

"Mona!" I cried, rushing over to her.

And then she did a strange thing, unlike anything she had done before or would do over those last few days she remained with me. She put her arms around me and rocked me, shushing me as though I were a small child. As we stood there, her rocking me gently and running her fingers through my shamelessly thin, greasy hair, I stared at the bulging contours of the sheet draped across her shrine. And as I listened, it was almost as though her wordless whispers were rising from the things she had hidden away there.

Then we made love—for what turned out to be the last time. When it was over I buried my face between her cheek and shoulder and fell into an unsettling sleep that was disturbed by a series of sharp stomach cramps. I tossed and turned, trying to force my eyes open, gradually becoming aware that the pains I was feeling were something more than those of a simple stomach ache. Something was burrowing into my body and tearing it apart, breaking through my rib cage and devouring my heart, my lungs ... everything inside that twisting, struggling cavity. Though my eyes were still not open, I was able to see the thing that was eating me. It glared at me, shreds of meat hanging out of its bloody mouth.

Mona.

I awoke screaming. I sat up in bed and looked over to the kitchenette light, the only light on in the apartment. There, drowning out my single scream with its constant, hideous cries was an animal—not much different from the one I'd seen struggle in the depths of that shallow pool on Lower Wacker—stretched out upon the kitchen table, thrashing furiously beneath the slender young woman who dug through its flesh with her teeth and claws.

"Mona ..." I croaked, as a piece of the transparent beast was ripped from its body and flung across the room. A small bit of it stuck to my cheek and I collapsed onto the sheets, trying to rub the hot, steaming mass from my face. I pulled the covers over my head and tried to wake up, realizing that the stomach pains had disappeared without a trace, as though they had belonged to someone else all along.

When I rose the next morning Mona was gone. I examined the kitchenette thoroughly, trying to find traces of the gruesome feeding I'd witnessed the night before, but there was no sign of a struggle, just the usual clutter on the table. I felt the spot on my cheek where the glutinous flesh had splattered me and remembered that elusive oily sensation I had felt on my first day I'd walked through the motionless array of Shabbies.

Then I heard it. A familiar ringing noise that seemed to snake through the air, stinging my skin and jabbing into my ears like a long needle.

I turned to the corner where Mona's secret shrine lay. As I stepped toward it, I could feel the pressure of that invisible fluid closing in around me again. I knelt and placed my hand on the sheet. It was warm, its surface like silk; and when I ran my hand across the gentle luxurious folds in the fabric, it sighed and twisted like reacting flesh.

When I yanked the sheet aside I didn't see the mosaic of clutter, but an emptiness, black and cold. A stench rose from that emptiness, and with it invisible clouds of oil that struck at my face and hands. I let the sheet drop back into place. Its movement was slow and graceful and did not end until it stretched and spasmed, letting out a quivering sigh as it finally stopped.

I touched my face and my hand came away with a layer of transparent ooze that grew warmer and warmer the longer it remained in contact with my skin.

IV

Her last few days in the apartment were a nightmare for me. She was in and out all the time, leaving each time as though she would never return, and later walking back in the door as though returning had been an unforgivable failure of nerve. It was no longer as though she didn't know I existed; it was as though she were suddenly so aware of my presence, so appalled by it, that she had to keep moving and distracting herself to keep from being overcome by it.

The warm weather that had brought the Shabbies from whatever realm they ordinarily inhabited would be returning in a matter of weeks and so, I believed from Mona's nervous manner, would the Shabbies. I knew that every time she walked out the door could easily mark the last moment I would ever see her.

Finally, one especially frigid night, she opened the door and cast a hateful, unregretting glare in my direction. I was sure that the time had finally come. I broke down and ran to the door, slamming it and whirling her around to face me.

"Mona. Please ..."

She averted her eyes and tried to slip quickly past me. I grabbed her by the shoulders and fought her sudden thrashing, but her strength and her will to resist were far greater than I had expected. I found myself literally trying to tackle her, pull her down to the floor. I was willing to kill her just so that she might have to look me in the eyes. Mona shrieked and wailed as she had on that evening on Lower Wacker Drive when the Shabbie tried to wrestle her to the ground for what were probably the exact same reasons.

She struck me across the face. I could feel the blood spreading down my cheek. I struck her next blow aside and backed away.

I called her Mona one last time.

And then she attacked. It was all a blur, the hazy, fading end of it a frail human girl, the harder, onrushing, leading edge of something ugly and ferocious—rows of twitching, flickering blades mounted on glutinous, transparent cords of flesh. I covered my face with folded arms and dropped to the floor as a thousand needlepoints pierced and broke off inside my skin. I felt a sprinkle of cool water, then heard the door slam.

I lay there for quite some time, afraid to move. When I finally sat up, it was dark, and Mona was gone.

My skin was clean and unbroken.

I tried to sleep that night, but every time I closed my eyes I was struck again by the image of that girl zooming forward through the haze, her face turning into a grotesque, glass-flesh monster, mouth open and ready to tear me to shreds. I didn't want to know what my dreams would have made of such a vision, and ended up going to work the next morning with no sleep whatsoever. I didn't sleep the next night either, only nodding off occasionally on the train for the next three days, until on the fourth night sleep finally beat me into submission.

I avoided Lower Wacker and spent as little time in the apartment as I could; and when I did, I prevented my eyes from coming to rest on that corner of hers.

Did I really believe she wasn't coming back? It was only in my most agonizing moments that I actually convinced myself I was really in love with Mona and not merely a slave to the presence she had offered me as an antidote to my suffocating loneliness. I began to fantasize that she returned to me in the guise of a shy, repentant but otherwise quite normal woman who would speak to me and not only heal all my wounds and explain away all my madness.

It was this hope, pierced with a lifetime's worth of bitterness, that ruined me in the end.

I lost my job. Various reasons were given for my abrupt termination, but the real reasons were obvious and plentiful. I no longer bathed. I rarely changed my clothes. I talked to myself. Sometimes I talked to Mona. And sometimes I just wept for her, in loud but stifled gasps.

On the night I lost my job, I returned to the apartment in a rage. I looked at the shambles I had made of it since I'd frightened Mona away: dirty clothes strewn and wadded across every surface, half-eaten food festering away on the floor and tabletops, magazines opened and tossed across furniture as though I were always in the middle of reading a dozen different useless articles and advertisements. The TV had remained on for three weeks, until the picture fizzled out and I was left with no more than twenty-four hours of static. I felt another useless bout of crying coming over me.

No, not again. No more.

I let out a scream and proceeded to tear the place apart. Why not finish the job since it seemed to be what my body really wanted to do? I tore up clothes and magazines, emptied the contents of my refrigerator and freezer across every surface upon which those contents could land or stick.

And then I tore the old sheet away from Mona's corner. I was struck by the insane logic that made it look like so much more than a mere collection of garbage. I began tearing away at the complex, symmetrical formation she had created, hurling rusted metal, grime-coated shards of glass, rat and pigeon corpses, and completely unidentifiable, convoluted masses of slick or hairy or sharp material across my room, so that what had once been a carefully but enigmatically constructed puzzle was no more than a scattered addition to the wasteland of clutter and crap that had once been my apartment.

But within days, the apartment was clean and barren and lifeless. I, too, had grown clean and barren and lifeless. I took showers until I was red and raw, and though I stared out my windows for hours on end, I did not leave the place for over a week.

When I finally did, it was to take a train downtown and revisit my old haunts: Lower Wacker Drive, the crossroads of my former life. It was early April now, and the weather had that cruel, unpredictable bite Chicago weather always has in spring along the lakefront: cold or warm—not merely on one frustrating day to the next—but from one gust of wind to another, from one patch of light to the adjacent shadow.

And there they were. I don't know why it surprised me so much. Only three of them, standing brittle and motionless, as though just barely focusing their translucent flesh into this world. Upon first seeing the three thin and ragged men, all their attention centered inward on some kind of transitional pain, I felt as though I could have stepped right through them and they would have collapsed—like water escaping through an abruptly ruptured membrane. I sat on the catwalk and watched them for several hours, waiting for a sign of movement—of life just waiting for something that might be a clue, a signpost that would lead me to my Mona.

But as the rush hour began on the streets above, some of it spilled down onto Lower Wacker and people began to pass by on their way home. They didn't seem to notice the three Shabbies at all. Instead they focused on me, sitting pensive and alone, a very clean but ragged man on a filthy catwalk.

I kept coming back. Soon I began to read those unsettling stares and glances of pity and revulsion on the faces of the passersby and realized that they thought I was just another homeless resident of Lower Wacker Drive. But of course I had a definite purpose. I was watching the Shabbies, watching their numbers increase slowly and steadily, watching as they came gradually into focus and began moving around, transparent and iridescent at first, but nearly solid, nearly corporeal as the weeks progressed. I walked among them, trying to follow—to imitate—their seemingly random patterns, listening to them speak to one another in those rapid, wordless whispers, and occasionally looking one in the eye and have him return my stare, and acknowledge my existence with a nod of the head or with that unsettling stretch of the facial muscles that I had seen so often in Mona, that grimace I had always told myself was a smile.

Soon there were dozens of them, milling about a stretch of Lower Wacker Drive that was just over three blocks long. The police would drive by, sometimes lean out the windows, but they seemed incapable of seeing the Shabbies for what they really were. So did the muddled and preoccupied commuters. The transients who haunted Lower Wacker feared them too much to get close and see what the Shabbies really were, or feel the tension their presence created on the thin, wet fabric of our world. When I arrived in the morning I would feel the warm, oily hug of the membrane as it closed in on me, greasing me as though to ease my passage into the great dark otherspace where Mona hid from me, not knowing how much I needed her, missed her.

Eventually I could no longer return home. I had to stay down there with them, knowing that they could disappear at any moment, knowing that when the time came, I would have to be there with them, ready to cross over with them, ready to face Mona again and make her understand.

I began to think of myself as a Shabbie. I told myself that my clothes and the pallor of my skin were beginning to resemble theirs, that when I spoke to them they were no longer merely words but part of that deeper, hushed language the Shabbies used themselves, that when Mona's thousand needlepoints had pierced me just before her departure, she had passed some of that essence into me.

But the Shabbies could not understand me and I could not understand them. And when I was hungry, I had to buy something to eat—at first with my dwindling supply of ready cash, and when that was gone, with money I could squeeze from the people on the streets above me. The Shabbies merely disappeared—only a few at a time—and would return gorged, the stripped limbs of lesser creatures dangling from their hands.

One very cold October morning they began to migrate. I followed them as they marched toward lower Michigan Avenue, feeling the tug of the oily strands that brushed and bathed me, anointed me and, finally, held me back as the Shabbies began to disperse before my eyes, spreading out as weightless globlets of amber fluid, scattering into smaller and smaller droplets until they were no more than a mist.

When it seemed I was all alone I turned and saw one last Shabbie, a young woman who looked not much different than Mona had on her first day. I called her Mona but she did not respond. I could already see the frayed threads of her clothes pulling apart, waving like the cilia of smaller and smaller drifting organisms, her transparent flesh and the tissues underneath softening for the final diffusion.

I leaped at her, crying out. I caught a hot wave of the sweet smelling flesh and felt it rupture and collapse around me. I fell to the street, sobbing out that name over and over again.

When I finally gathered myself and trudged toward the nearest stairway, I thought about my apartment, wondering whether I had been gone so long that it had been rented out from under me, whether I could even remember enough about the world up there to reintegrate myself into the margins where I'd once lived my life.

I made it to the top of the stairs and scanned the passing crowds. I breathed in the October city gases and felt the winds slap and sting at my dry, brittle flesh and the whispers of bitter cold darkness that seeped in toward my shabby soul.

THE BIG OL' CLOWN LADY

I was negotiating my way through the crowds at my ten year high school reunion, trying to establish or avoid eye contact as the situation dictated, trying to find as many different ways as I could to say the same things about myself to everyone I met, trying not to be smug or spiteful and trying not to notice these same attitudes in those I saw and spoke to—when someone, I don't know who, mentioned her name.

The Big Ol' Clown Lady.

I turned around, thinking it would be an old friend of mine, but I couldn't match the voice with any that I heard in the conversational niches surrounding me. I tried to shrug it off and get back into the momentum of the proceedings. But soon I realized there was no momentum. Not for me.

So I went out to the lobby and phoned Carla to see if she was feeling any better and to tell her what an awful time I was having without her. But even as I talked I could feel myself drifting. To Carla I probably just sounded a little drunk. After I hung up and slouched in the doorway, watching the reunion, I felt myself drawn away from this banquet hall, this body, this time. Suddenly, a memory dormant for twenty years was cracking through the plaque built up over my childhood. So I left, went back to the motel room with a bottle of Scotch and a bucket of ice and just let the memory break on through…

The Big Ol' Clown Lady.

Ours had once been a small town surrounded by a thriving patchwork of family farms. Most newcomers were drawn there by the commuter line into the city, the new housing developments, the new schools, the new mall. I was four years old when we moved there. Even at that age, so new and fresh to the town... to the world, I can remember seeing her in her layers of brown rags, shambling about the streets like some great, hulking Pliocene ground sloth, talking and singing to herself, leading a swarm of chattering insects, dragging her long canvas sacks behind her, filling the air with an aroma that to me, at that time, seemed to suggest not so much filth and decomposition and illness as it did a kind of mystery—the exotic, alien realm in which she dwelled.

Once I entered school, I realized that everyone knew who the Big Ol' Clown Lady was, with her wide, weathered face laced with warts and always painted into a nightmarish caricature of an exotic model, lips and cheeks all red, eyes trapped in the center of deep black pits. Kids told stories about her, threw stuff at her, and referred to her in all kinds of oaths and threats.

Off Route 31, in the long grasses that edged the forest, she lived in an old tanker. Its door was a jagged opening that twisted and stretched so far across the rust-covered cylinder that the whole place seemed ready to collapse. Surrounding it was her...I still don't know what to call it. From the road it looked like heaps of trash half-hidden amid the weeds. From behind the big rock where we used to sit sometimes and watch her, waiting to see if we might witness one of the hideous and otherwise unbelievable actions attributed to her, it looked like a garden of robust, thorned plants that were twisted into what looked almost like human figures. And the contorted forms of these plants were mirrored in the strange statues that stood among them. Built from obscurely worked bits of garbage, these figures seemed to stand watch around her rusted tanker, ready to leap into life were we to step out from behind the rock...

Once I saw a boy strike her in the face with a thrown pop can. As she rubbed her cheek, she glared with menacing eyes at the boy and moved on. It was whispered for weeks afterward that this boy, a notorious eleven-year-old bully, would one night be dragged from his bed and minced into the Big Ol' Clown Lady's cauldron, which was rumored to sit bubbling with an unspeakable stew at all times.

When, six months later, a different boy actually did disappear while on a Cub Scout outing, we all knew his real fate...and whose crime he'd been made to pay for. No adult seemed astute enough to follow up on this idea, however, and in the news reports that made it to television her name was never mentioned.

Two weeks before I began the third grade, my mother died in a head-on collision on Route 31. My father—still a very young man—was delirious with grief, and for months afterwards was subject to sudden fits of weeping. With the assistance of visiting relatives and neighbors, my father and I were separated with an almost clinical efficiency. I would go directly to our neighbor Mrs. Carver's house after school, where my Aunt Paulina would pick me up late in the evening and take me home, to find my father sitting, brittle and listless, trying to reach out to me from across the cold abyss between us but never able to do more than smile and joke feebly with me in a reedy voice that sounded less and less familiar every day. I wondered, as September darkened into October, whether any sort of normality would ever return to our lives, whether Aunt Paulina would ever go home, whether my father and I would ever be alone together again—whether my father would even live out the fall and winter.

It was a warm Friday afternoon in late October when two friends and I went to a gas station on the edge of the old downtown to buy bottles of pop out of the machine in front. It was a weekly ritual carried over from the summer idyll. We sat on the curb and listened to the foul-mouthed banter of the two farm boys who manned the gas pumps. On this day I was haunted by a dream I'd had the night before in which my father—withered into a leathery corpse—took me out on an ominous sea in a rickety boat. He told me that my mother was one of the birds of prey that circled and squawked over our boat, and that if we couldn't find a way to trick her back into her grave, she would surely devour us.

I dreaded the sight of old Mrs. Carver, Aunt Paulina, and today—especially today— my father, so when my friends got up to leave I just sat there, thinking, trying to wedge something opaque between me and my dreams.

When one of the farm boys kicked my leg and told me I better be moving on, I sulked away with head down and hands in pockets, still trying to drive two images out of my head: the slight glimmer deep within the empty eye sockets of my father's face and the hideous grin on that bird face that kept swooping down at us in my dream.

It was an abrupt collision. She didn't see me and I hadn't seen her. I seemed to sink deep into the soft, dank layers of rags before I bounced back and fell on my butt, palms slapping the pavement. There, on her knees, staring at me from behind the caked and crackling fields of red and black make-up, was the Big Ol' Clown Lady, sputtering a stream of indecipherable curses. As she rose to her feet she feigned a lunge at me, cackling with laughter when I jumped back with a yelp. Then she stopped to pick up the garbage that had spilled out of her canvas sack in our collision. I just stood there, watching the gigantic brown back bobbing and the fat, scarred and warted hands pulling together the rags, bundled book pages, bottles and cans. She gave me one last look—surprised that I should still be standing there, then she limped on, away from downtown and out towards Route 31.

When I stepped away, I kicked something into the street. It was a twisted, rusted scrap of metal that I realized must have fallen out of her sack. I picked it up and discovered that, in its intricate patterns, with its soft, membranous patches hidden deep within those patterns, it was far more than the rusted old can I had taken it for. As I held it close I heard a high-pitched fluttering from within.

I turned and saw the hulking back of the Big Ol' Clown Lady turning onto Route 31. But as I watched her, I felt something wet slither and shiver in my palm. When I looked at the thing in my hand it had somehow changed its shape. Moisture was condensing along the thickest of its strands. Beads of water lined up in single file along each wrinkle. And now it felt less like rusted metal as it seemed to be dripping, leaking into my palm, soft and limp like a soaked chamois.

When I turned back to the retreating old woman, the fluttering whistle dropped into a mournful sigh. Without a thought, I began to follow her.

I was half a mile from the gas station when I first thought of Mrs. Carver and Aunt Paulina and how worried they would be if I didn't show up at Mrs. Carver's. But why was I following the Big Ol' Clown Lady? It would have been no use asking me— better instead to ask the sweating, restless thing in my hand, a thing I now refused to look at. There was no doubt that it was homing in with a desperate urgency along the same course as the Big Ol' Clown Lady. As long as I held it in my hand I was no more than its mode of transport. I held it as tightly as it held on to me.

Because of her slow, shambling gait and because I ran part of the way, I caught up to within twenty paces behind her. If she knew I was there she took no notice. She never turned or hurried or hesitated. When she veered off the gravel and onto the weed-lined path and I came to grips with my destination, I hesitated, standing along the edge of the road and watching as she passed by the rock beyond which none of us had ever dared to venture. But the thing in my hand hugged and pinched at me, and I was forced to take a step, and then another, down onto the path, beyond the shelter of the rock, out to where the weeds stood about like tall, twisted sentinals. The tortured stature of these guards was echoed by the mounds of trash that seemed to be impaled by and cemented onto thin rusted armatures, scarecrows that lured swarms of the biggest flies I had ever seen. When I stepped too close to one of these figures, an insect slapped my cheek, shrieking as it bounced away.

I saw her disappear into the jagged tear that served as a door on her oil tanker. I stopped again. A stream of foul air rushed out from that black interior. The dread within me exploded out of my mouth and eyes as I looked at the rusted patches and streaks that stretched over the surface of that tanker. I turned away, trying to move my legs back in the direction from which they'd come. My hand and then my whole arm were raised against my will, and with my face averted, I was led by the thing on the end of that arm. We stepped through the rusty, jagged lips and stood in the black stench within. It was nothing like I had imagined it to be—no cauldron, no children's skulls. It was a claustrophobic enclosure that reflected no light whatsoever, as though the tear had sealed shut behind me. I looked behind me, and the light that had delineated the edges of the tear was gone. When I turned back there was another, smaller tear in the metal, and through this opening shone an ominous, brown-red light. The sky was the wrong color.

We decided to step through this tear.

As I stood now in this new realm, I saw pools of vapor and fluid float along the wrinkled surface of the canopied sky. I saw a panoply of crimson-tinted weeds lining the path and the grimaces formed by the petals of their flowers. Above and around me flew things that may have been birds or may have been large insects, or may have been something else entirely.

Lost within this riotous foliage were the armatures, covered with garbage and muscle—like twisted human figures, reduced to foodstuff for the things that swarmed on them.

I began to see patches of bone and meat, scattered remnants of humans and other animals, and the reflective carapaces of thousands of tiny creatures feeding on that meat, chattering away as they dug their faces boneward.

The path I was following led up an incline, a hill on which sat a single regal figure—the Big Ol' Clown Lady—her rags now glimmering, the frayed threads alive and alert and waving from their fabric beds like a swarm of aquatic worms.

She was feeding as I approached her. As I climbed the hill I saw a metal armature peering over her shoulder. The iridescent carapaces of thousands of flies created the illusion that flesh was bubbling to life and spreading over the rusted skeleton.

She was eating an arm, a small arm with a Band-Aid over the knuckle of the middle finger, a Band-Aid with an oil smudge on it, where I had brushed it on the pavement in my fall in front of the gas station. I looked at my free arm and hand, then at the arm from which she fed, identical in every way except that the one she was holding was torn away at the elbow, and beneath the skin there was not me, my mind, my immortal soul, only meager strands of raw meat.

She looked at me with tiny, sunken eyes, folds deepening over them as her face contorted, flashing her crooked, bloody teeth and hissing. She threw the arm down and reached for a thatch of hair that was connected to the severed head of a boy. I looked at that face and thought, *so this is what I look like with my eyes shut.* And in the instant I thought that, the eyes opened and looked straight at me, as two rows of crooked teeth sank into the cheek and pulled at it. As she tugged, the skin tore and I saw a line running up towards one of those open eyes, and I thought: no, please God, not my eyelids...

I shrieked when I saw her head jerk back, pulling the skin free. She smiled at me through her painted, bloodied face and held the head for me to see.

The thing wrapped around my hand squeezed my wrist. I had actually forgotten about it. Now I held it out to her. It went limp in my hand, a blood-dripping mass of flesh.

She looked at it, shocked, and then back at me, her whole expression changed, as though reading every thought, every memory out of me. She set the head down gently and reached with slow, trembling fingers as the thing stretched away from my hand and towards hers.

The transfer of that flesh, from my hand to hers, left me trembling in inexplicable ecstasy. She laughed to watch me quiver, and I saw, beneath all that paint, the blood and madness, a flicker of tenderness. These two—my orgasm and her glimmer of recognition afterwards, were to take me years to identify and understand, to a time when the event was no more than a dim, dreamlike half-memory.

She took that dripping slab I handed her and tossed it over her shoulder, where it smacked into and wrapped around the top of the armature. The flies all dropped or flew away, and the armature pulsed into motion as the slab took on the shape of a face.

Its eyes opened, looked down at me, stealing my attention.

"You! Boy! What do you see all around you? *Food!* Remember this! Your mind is the prisoner of your flesh, and of the flesh of whatever will one day eat you as well as everything you have ever eaten. Food, boy! Next time you think of your mother, ask yourself what is eating her in her wet, soily pit and what it's chosen to do with all those thoughts of hers."

And then the sinewy face exploded with laughter.

"Now! Go home and eat your dinner!"

I looked away, back to where the Big Ol' Clown Lady had been sitting, to where the pile of dismembered limbs—mine—had rested at her feet, but there was only another rusted, garbage-laced armature; twisted, headless, lifeless. I looked back up at the talking face, but it too was dead, lost beneath the swarm of feasting flies.

I stumbled back down the hill, cowering beneath the screeching, wrinkled, milk-clouded canopy of a sky, averting my eyes from all that scattered, thinking meat, my mind whirling too fast to rest on a single thought. I worked my way along the path, trying to narrow my tear-clouded vision down to the piece of path where my foot would land next, trying to drown out all that buzzing and screeching with the sounds of my weeping. Occasionally something big would swoop near me and I'd feel the brush of its wings and think of my mother and the bird she had turned into in my dream.

Soon I heard a rumble, a drone. Cars, moving down Route 31. I looked around me. I held up my arms and examined them. I was whole and alive and it was getting dark.

I moved quickly along the road after that, knowing I was in trouble, knowing that I had no excuse, no explanation, for my absence. But as I hurried, I began to realize that, of course, there was no need to worry. My experience... down there, had been a dream, this hurrying, the realization itself... it was all a dream. And as I drew closer to home, to the light in Mrs. Carver's living room, I began to comprehend the vastness of the dream, realizing that all of this, extending—*of course!*—back to my mother's death, was a dream, from which my mother herself would awaken me.

But once inside Mrs. Carver's house, examining the stress and anger on the faces of Mrs. Carver, Aunt Paulina, and my father, feeling the depth and the resilience of the illusion surrounding me, I began to fear that the dream wasn't going to let go of me at all.

Which, of course, it did not. By the time I began to accept the idea that my mother was truly dead and buried and that her death was not just a dream, I had nearly forgotten the events that had triggered the conviction in the first place. I saw the Big Ol' Clown Lady again, frequently for a time, but less and less as she grew older and less able to move around town. I always felt extreme physical discomfort upon seeing her, but I suspect now that through most of that time I did not understand why.

Nor could I understand, lying there with my empty Scotch bottle, in my buzzing motel room, why the mention of her name should, twenty years later, bring this strange memory gushing before my mind's eye. But gush it did, as I sprawled there in the dark, the room spinning in one direction, my body spinning in the other, while the darkness filled with visions of that secret realm the Big Ol' Clown Lady had once shared with me.

The next morning, hung over, depressed, lonely for my sweet wife whom I should never have left back at home, I checked out of my room and shambled to my car. I took a drive through town, past my old house and through subdivisions that used to be the farms and fields that had once separated us from the outside world. Somehow, I ended up on Route 31, moving ever farther from the expressway ramp that would lead me home. I had to see… had to know that even there, the relentless march of development had left its paved, uniform traces.

But there it was, an outrageous incongruity, more overgrown with weeds than ever, as though it was trying to disguise itself as part of the forest preserve that it had once framed. I pulled the car over, got out and just stood there, searching for the path.

I found it, and farther along found what I was sure was the rock we used to hide behind. How small we must have been for three of us to hide comfortably behind it. And then I went beyond the rock, where the weeds and trees seemed to blend into a pained, twisted landscape of crippled limbs and razor-toothed leaves. Had a botanist ever wandered through this horrifying latticework? Hadn't anyone ever noticed that here, along this stretch of land, grew plants that surely grew nowhere else in the world?

I scraped my jacket against a sharp tooth of rusted metal. It was one of the armatures, a bare metal statue, nearly swallowed within the trunk of the black, twisting tree. I looked around me. They were everywhere, mirroring both the shapes of men and the plant life around them. But they were small, and it was clear that they resembled humans far less than they did the trees. Would I have even made this comparison had I not felt... known... of their secret nature?

The path led me directly to an open, desolate patch of ground, where I came upon an almost flattened sheet of rust, all that was left of the tanker, aside from the tiny scattered specks of rust, ground into the gray earth.

I wandered back along the path, the whole experience and the memory that triggered it now overwhelmed by my hangover. I stopped and vomited up my entire breakfast. When I finished, I had a throbbing headache. I looked around. I was on the wrong path. No matter, I supposed, I could still see Route 31 through the branches.

A bit farther on, I came across a bulldozer, tilted onto its side. Weeds spread over it and a gnarled tree sprouted up through the cab. Rust spread across the surface, radiating like millions of capillaries, so that where the capillaries had not thickened into solid patches, it appeared almost like a delicate, bloodshot membrane.

Within the darkness of that cab from, I thought I heard a sound. I approached and peered down through the broken glass, trying to identify that sound—when something flew out, striking my cheek. The sound continued, louder even as I moved further and more quickly away from that abandoned bulldozer.

I stumbled and fell atop a cracked slab of concrete. I stood, brushed myself off and took a good hard look around me. There were more of these slabs here, and another overturned bulldozer, its surface rusting away in complex, intertwining strands.

So they had tried. Perhaps more than once. What could possibly have happened here to stop them?

Her voice hit me like a wave, scraping through the rubble and concrete, hissing through the vegetation. Laughing at me...

I ran. I refused to look behind me, refused to look up at the sky that had been casting a gray pallor all morning but which now seemed to be turning the world into a sienna haze. I refused to acknowledge the swarms of insects that were erupting at my feet, slashing against me as they rose, their buzzing harmonizing with the laughter that chased me.

I could see Route 31 up ahead, but was I getting any closer? For a time, as the laughter got louder and the eruption of bugs grew thicker, the highway actually seemed to be receding. But then, just as I had on an afternoon twenty years before, I burst through the membrane and rose up onto the flat surface of the old highway. I leaned against the car and retched up... something. Had I been swallowing those bugs?

As I got in my car I noticed a sign that I had not seen before. It informed interested parties that this land was for sale. It had probably once provided the phone number to call, but the sign was being swallowed by monstrous weeds hugged at it from every side, threatening to pull it down into the depths of the Big Ol' Clown Lady's blight.

I turned the car around and drove down Route 31 towards the expressway. All around me were new subdivisions and shopping facilities and beautifully landscaped corporate headquarters. I kept telling myself, "See? See how tenacious we are? We build and overrun and wipe out and overcome..."

But Route 31 was an old road, potholed, whole slabs of it crackling away, and small black twisted things grew inconspicuously along the edges...

Someday, of course, that blight would be bulldozed away, muscled out of existence and replaced by a mall, a country club, a housing development. Wouldn't it? How could it not be? How could it continue to grow thicker and darker and more out of place, when civilization was edging up against it, hungry for the land?

I tried to tell myself it would as I raced down the expressway, looking in the rearview mirror constantly to assure myself that nothing was following me.

But something was wrong with the hood of my car, my six-month-old Buick Regal. The front end was decaying, and that decay was reaching out towards me, across the hood, like millions of tiny capillaries.

They didn't look much different from the trails of blood I saw whenever I looked at myself in the rearview mirror, blood that trickled and smeared and puddled across the meat of my horrified face.

THE HIVE

There were more than a dozen of us. When the midday sun filled the Hive with amber light, we were an army, running and howling over the flagstone floor of the courtyard, beyond the grip of our parents and immune to the retreating shadows.

But at night those same shadows would advance and we would retreat, hugging the pant legs of our mothers or fathers or whomever of our elders we could trust in the darkness. We became dependent on the protection of these loving giants who ignored the hunger that lived in the shadows, who triumphed in the apparent silliness of our terror. We were children, after all.

And if every once in a while one of us came screaming to our mothers with blood-soaked splinters in our skin, it was because somehow—in ways they did not bother to construe and we were too small to comprehend—we had been bad.

It is the earliest family vacation I can remember. I was four years old, an only child, and my mother had told me I would be spending my days playing with other children—my cousins. I would meet my grandparents as well as aunts and uncles who'd heard all about me and were dying to meet me. I would play on the same stones and under that same tree as my mother had so many summers of her own childhood. And if my mother seemed to twitch a little as she told me these things, how could I suspect it was because she was afraid: for me, for herself, of her own memories. And if my parents fought almost the entire drive, then it was only because my father didn't really care whether I had fun with my cousins or not.

That drive took an entire day, and by the time we arrived at the Hive, it was dark and I had already been asleep for hours.

As my father carried me in his arms, I awoke to see more stars in the sky than I had ever seen in my life. The night was so loud with the calls of bugs and birds and dogs, it was hard to imagine those cries were coming from the surrounding forest—which after all was no more than a distant, uniform blackness. Maybe all those animals were calling down to us from the stars. The universe was immense, and yet—in my grogginess and in the warm protective grip of my father—so intimate. I imagined all those creatures perched on stars, babbling away, talking about me: *Look, there he is now. Do you think he can hear us?*

Compared to that display, the shapeless black mound we were approaching was too insignificant to warrant my attention. I rubbed the top of my head against my father's neck and laughed a sleepy, satisfied laugh.

And then we were inside. Here the darkness was deep and intrusive, and the light searing and unkind. I shut my eyes, but I continued to listen: to the whispers, to the shouts, to the clatter of shoes on wood and stone, to the hum of electric lights, to the creaks and groans of the Hive itself.

As I pretended to sleep, I felt myself poked, heard the cooing of adults swarming around me. I was afraid my father would let go of me, relinquish me to one of those hissing, ogling strangers. I was not too young to sense that their attentions towards me were somehow proprietary. I shut my eyes tighter, clutched my father more ferociously.

In response, they all laughed.

I had never been around so many children. There were babies and wobbly toddlers, but they were kept out of our reach and didn't interest us anyway. Because of those babies, and because our parents were so preoccupied with each other and with all the old people who lived in the Hive, my cousins really did run wild and unattended. I was the youngest allowed to run with the other children, and so I occupied a position of some distinction: though bullied by some, I was under the protection of most. I was the easiest to carry and to lift into the lowest tree branches, and I could fit into the narrowest, most inaccessible passageways.

Seen from inside, the Hive seemed enormous to me, a self-contained world. How could a house be so gigantic? And yet, it wasn't really a house at all, but rather a nearly circular fortress with a spacious courtyard at its center. Nested within its great outer wall and extending along three-quarters of its circumference was a double row of tiny, unconnected one-and-two-room houses. Running between the rows of houses was a real street, a patchwork of wood planks and flagstones. This covered avenue could be accessed from two entrances, one at each end of its extremes. One was wide and bright and inviting. Just inside this entrance were the houses in which my parents and I and all of my cousins were staying. The other entrance was dark and rank with the smell of decay.

Along most of its length this avenue was wired with light. But as one moved deeper, the light dimmed until the houses were lost in darkness. Here the windows and doors were broken or rotted away. We would march down the center of the avenue, holding hands, leaning into each other, toying with our fear as we neared the avenue's darkest stretches. We teased the darkness. Smelled the rot.

And listened.

For this is where we heard the voices, the groaning and grinding of the things that lived in the wood. The first time I went on one of these expeditions I cried the whole way down the avenue, not because of what I heard or saw or anticipated but simply because everyone else, even the oldest among us, was so afraid. I was too young *not* to know better. We were here *because* it scared us. We stepped up to and even into the darkness because something—I'm not sure if any us knew what—could happen to us if we ventured too far.

I had the unshakable fear that whenever the lights above flickered, they were about to flicker out for good, plunging the avenue into darkness. I was sure that in the dark and the rot would spread like fire, back down the way we'd come.

Out of the crooked window of our own little house we could see the center courtyard and the Great Tree. We heard the chatter of my aunts and uncles and cousins, who were staying in houses near our own.

Farther down was the house of our grandparents, more rundown than ours, the lights dimmer and more untrustworthy. Deeper into darkness the houses were even more decayed, their occupants more ancient and forbidding. They would invite us inside, sometimes with their words nearly lost within death-rattle wheezes, or sometimes with whispered lullabies that made my skin crawl. And their hand motions were always so crude, so stiff and puppet-like, they confirmed something I had always suspected of the world but had never been able to verify until now: the reality of certain people or things was dependent on how wide my eyes were open when I looked at them, and whether I was sleepy or afraid or sick to my stomach.

The centerpiece of our world was that great, all-encompassing tree. Not only did it seem to be the most gigantic living thing in all creation, but I was convinced that it was truly conscious of my presence, and of my almost constant need for reassurance. It was warm to the touch in the same way my parents were warm to the touch—a purposeful, protective radiation. Did I say it was the centerpiece of our world? No, that isn't quite true. Because it bathed me in its radiance, I was sure, as I had never been and as I would never be again, that *I* was the centerpiece of the world. My parents had always treated me as though I were the single most significant part of their lives, but I was beginning to sense their occasional distraction, their irritation. The tree seemed to care for nothing but me, and recognized and magnified my importance.

We loved to play beneath the tree, to bathe in the sunlight it filtered upon us, to climb those accommodating branches. We would search out its soft, moist places, where we would rest our palms, our cheeks, and listen for those intoxicating atmospheric disturbances that were beyond mere sound. And it was high in those branches that the world of our parents and all the pains and failures that filled our fragile little lives faded out of existence. The tree was the world, its branches the continents, its leaves the oceans and we … its attendant angels.

In spite of this, the tree was contained fully inside the Hive. The tree anchored itself to the inward-sloping walls, it pushed against the chaotic patchwork of amber-colored glass that made up the ceiling above it. But the tree's thin, winding extremities were no match for the Hive that surrounded it. And because the tree was so clearly ours, and the Hive so clearly our parents' and grandparents', I could not look at those branches, twisted and flattened against the glass and wood above us, without feeling the anger of tested loyalty. If the tree was a prisoner of the Hive, then so were we.

At night, when the tree grew cold and indifferent, I would turn to my parents. I'd wait for that moment when one or the other of them was free to cuddle and indulge me. At night, the three of us finally alone together in our tiny two-room house, I could feel the stress between them. My father wanted to leave, wanted to pack our bags and sneak away next morning before anyone awoke. He would argue with my mother, bringing it up again and again as though he couldn't remember having spoken about it a few minutes previously. "Not just yet," she would answer. And he would always want to know "Why?" She always had the same answer, repeated so often that sometimes I felt like answering his question myself. "Not until you talk to Grandfather," she'd say. I realize now she didn't mean our grandfather, but rather her own, a man I had yet to see, but of whose presence I was acutely aware.

Listening to their nightly bickering, I always sided with my father, because I thought that in the nighttime the Hive was the most frightening place in the entire world. But the next day, running across the flagstone courtyard or playing in and around the tree, I could think of nothing more wonderful than to spend the rest of my life in the Hive. Night and day then: the intoxication of one was canceled out entirely by the dread of the other, a dread that could only be cured by the dawn of a new day.

Throughout it all, I am sure I never once ventured outside. The walls around me, those branches, and those amber-colored filters above me, became the barriers of the known universe. The silhouetted forest and the starry sky that I had seen through sleepy eyes on the night of our arrival were just distant memories. I had exaggerated their scale and significance simply because I had not yet experienced the magnitude of the Hive or the all-consuming attentiveness of the tree.

And all the while, I was catching on to my father. He was afraid, and every day, just as my mother was growing more insistent, he was becoming more afraid. Sometimes, early in the morning or late in the evening, I would quietly follow him around the little house, observing his behavior. I could not then decipher the language his movements and expressions spoke, but replaying them now, I can read his despair, his suffocation. I project all that I have learned since onto the vision of him sitting at the table, palms together as though in prayer, poking and rubbing his fingers against the tip of his nose, his eyes wet, red and unblinking, staring somewhere far beyond the facing wall.

"Why don't you just go and talk to them?" she would say to him. "It isn't such a big deal. Just nod and smile and agree. If you want to leave so badly, just make a nice presentation of yourself, charm a smile or two out of them—you know you're capable of that—and then we can go. The approval of my family could mean a lot more than you think, somewhere down the line."

"Talk to who, Mommy?" I'd ask, planting myself between them, not so much curious as just reluctant to be ignored.

"Great-grandpa and great-uncle Henry, sweetheart. Daddy and I are talking. Why don't you go out on the porch and see if you can find the other children."

"You talk about them as though they were just …" His face would pinch with disgust. My father seemed to hate everybody there. "This place is wretched beyond words, Ellen. What is it we really want from them? Money? Approval? Or maybe, just protection from their disapproval? And what the hell do I have to do with it? Joey, buddy, why don't you go see if any of your cousins are out yet."

And so I would leave, and return hours later to the same bickering, which went on day after day and made no sense to me then and makes little more sense to me now. My mother and her family were in the thrall of a few old men, because they were the family patriarchs, because their love and approval was of unequaled significance to her, because theirs was a goodness that—no matter how cold and frightful—could not be ignored or contradicted. And because my father, her husband, was secondary to them. And because his intense dislike for them made him something less than secondary.

I no longer remember the name of the little girl who was eaten by the walls. I do remember very clearly what the girl looked like because I was, by virtue of my size, the one sent in to retrieve her.

On that morning, I was playing alone beneath the tree when I heard a commotion. My cousin Vincent Threadgil, a feral, snaggle-toothed nine-year-old, ran up and pointed to me. "You! Come with me!"

"What's going on?" I asked. But Vincent was already dragging me across the floor. He ignored the other children who crowded around us as we entered the avenue.

I began to panic. I tried to stop, tried to plant my feet and pull my arm from Vincent's grip. When he tugged at me, I began to cry. When he turned and began shouting at me, I started bawling. I was surrounded by older kids now, all of them shouting at me. I realize now that it was probably panic that made them so brutal, and my own panic that made their shouting seem so threatening. A teenage girl lifted me into the air and whisked me to a stretch of the avenue darker and more decrepit than I'd ever braved before. She put me down and pointed out the gap between two tiny houses, a narrow passage between two crooked walls, barely wide enough for me to fit. She hushed the other children and then kneeled before me, a pleading smile on her face. It wasn't much, but it was enough to stop my crying.

And in the relative quiet that followed, I heard a weak whimpering, emerging from that hostile cleft into which the girl was now directing my attention. Softly, she spoke the name of one of our female cousins. "She's back there and we can't get her to come out."

I looked at her, uncomprehending.

"None of us can fit back there," she stated firmly, so that there would be no doubt as to my mission.

"She's stuck?" I sniffled weakly.

The girl shook me. "You don't know that. You don't know that!" She took a deep breath and then smiled unsteadily when she saw I was about to start crying again. She ran a palm across my hair. "Just walk in there, go in and try to get her to come out. She won't even talk to us. But if you can reach her... you know... take her hand, maybe she'll come out."

"I got the flashlight," someone behind us said.

The girl gave me a little hug. In that moment she seemed almost magically beautiful. It was as though she knew she could bewitch me into doing this, and I could feel, quite suddenly, that yes, this would be all right. There would be light, there would be other kids watching to make sure nothing happened to me. Suddenly I was very important.

I stepped into a cold, narrow blackness, wading in and out of the path of the flashlight's quivering yellow eye. I had to step sideways to avoid fingerlets of wood angling out from the walls, and trust that the light would expose any jagged piece that might snag me.

I saw her quite suddenly, as the flashlight caught and wavered and then held on her. She was no more than three feet away, a pretty little blond girl not much bigger than me. She was looking right at me, probably had been throughout my entire journey to her. I tried to smile bravely, but realize now that she never saw any more than a silhouette of my head surrounded by that shaky halo.

I reached out for her hand. When she grasped mine, I noticed that the two walls were holding her head in a vise-grip. I realized this because in the moment we touched, the walls eased their grip on her and she was suddenly able to move her head freely. She gasped and blinked, and then began to weep.

I said, "Come on," or something equally consoling. I pulled on her hand, and began to step back the way I'd come. She took a first tentative step with me.

And then the walls clamped shut. I felt splinters strike my face, my arms, and especially the hand that held the girl's. I let go and watched as the walls closed around her, concealing her from view, though they didn't pen me in any tighter. I turned and ran, screaming and stumbling, tearing myself on the walls.

I could feel and hear chewing behind me and knew that at any moment I could be eaten as well.

I exploded out of the cleft, and hit the floor howling. I was still young enough to expect someone to pick me up after such a display, but though there were two or three times as many people there as before, not one came forward to console me. When I looked up I saw why.

He was the biggest man I had ever seen. That and the authority in his face seemed to dwarf everything around him. He was ancient, his skin a palimpsest upon which generations worth of scars, wrinkles and cancers were layered, converging into the characters of an unreadable alphabet. His eyes: icy blue glimmers from beneath eyebrows that cast shadows as deep as any in the Hive. His face seemed divided by a deep diagonal cleft, running from the temple to the opposite side of the chin. He looked at me for only an instant before I shut my eyes and turned my face to the floor.

It was the commotion that brought me to my feet in time to see the giant emerging from the same narrow gap in the walls. In his arms, the little girl, eyes open, limp, dirty and not nearly so pretty anymore. Considered what I'd seen in there, there was not much blood, but enough to send the girl's mother—just now pushing her way through the crowd—into hysterics so unbridled that half the children present began to cry. Someone grabbed me from behind and lifted me into the air. I screamed and kicked, even after I realized it was my own father.

He carried me out of the avenue and plopped me onto a stone bench in the courtyard, kneeling before me.

"What happened?" he asked, trying to calm his voice. He stroked my check and then examined his fingertips: blood.

He shuddered as he spoke. "Joey-boy, you wanna leave this place? You wanna get the heck out of this madhouse?"

I was ready to nod, but first looked over my father's shoulder at the tree, its branches so generous in their reach—outward to me, upward to the ceiling, to the walls. I lost interest in him, in what I'd just experienced in the walls, what I'd seen in the eyes of the old giant, and wondered quite abruptly if I should ask my father if I could sit in the tree awhile.

He shook me out of my reverie. "Joey? *Dammit!* Look at me, kid." His own eyes were red now and I had the most terrifying thought of all—my father was going to cry. Instead he carried me back to our bright, tiny house.

One morning soon afterwards, I awoke from an uneasy sleep, aware that my parents had been up all night fighting.

Whatever words passed between them, the upshot was certain: my father had given up. Smaller now, he looked as though he'd cried through most of the night. The courage he was working up in order to walk out that door and go meet with those old men was far weaker than the calm warmth with which he'd carried me into the Hive so many weeks ago.

And when he walked out our door he didn't look at my mother, and he didn't seem to hear me call out to him. I ran after him but the door shut in my face. In the rush of air that struck me I could smell the rot through which I'd walked in that narrow, wooden cleft only days before. It was then that I noticed our suitcases by the door, latched and standing, just waiting … .

My mother called my name, a cold, sharp insistence in her voice. I didn't want to turn and look into the face that could reduce my name to such a violent pair of syllables, but it seemed to be the only way to keep her from saying it again.

She was expressionless, her face oily and glimmering in the kitchen light. Though she glared in my direction, I knew she didn't see me.

"I want to go with him," I declared, my courage draining away by the time I reached the last two words.

"Your father will be fine. Stay and keep me company." A queer smile flitted across her face.

"I want to go away."

"We are going away."

"I want to go away with Daddy."

"We'll all leave together!" she hissed, squinting meanly at me. She looked like the old man who had gone into the wall to rescue the little girl. "Now, come sit with me."

Instead I ran, slamming the door as hard as I could behind me, as though I could somehow wedge it so she wouldn't be able to follow. It didn't matter. She probably never even got out of the chair.

I called to my father as I ran out to the courtyard. The tree seemed to move slightly as I passed it, to twist and to point my father out to me. He was standing at the ragged black mouth of the avenue.

"Daddy?" I cried, lunging into his arms. He lifted me high overhead and I shut my eyes and probably smiled. He shook me and pulled me close—but not for an embrace. When I opened my eyes he was glaring at me with an anguish that corrupted his features beyond recognition. He dropped to his knees and set me down, looking me in the eyes.

"What are you doing here?" he cried, shaking me with hands that suddenly seemed enormous. "Can't you people just … leave me alone? What the hell do I have to do?"

I had no answer. I didn't even know what he was talking about. I was bawling my eyes out, just trying to get away, not sure who I could go to now. Surely not my mother, and for the past few days there had been so few children, and so few adults I wasn't already afraid of.

There was only the tree.

He continued shouting at me but I could no longer hear him. I was just waiting for his grip to ease long enough for me to break free and run.

And then he pushed me to the ground. By the time I got to my feet, he was gone. Disappeared into the darkest stretch of the avenue, headed towards the house of my great-grandfather.

There were no children in the courtyard, only a thin gray man I had never seen before, leaning on a cane, glaring at me with hateful eyes.

I ran to the mouth of the avenue, but I passed our little house and kept running. I had no idea how I would ever face my mother, could no longer imagine what it would be like with either of them once we left the Hive. I kept on running, too clouded by tears and the sound of my sobbing to realize how quickly I'd passed beyond the range of bright lights. We children had always treaded the darkness cautiously, as though any thoughtless, impulsive movement would encourage something in the shadows—or perhaps the shadows themselves—to reach out and consume us. But I had already been consumed this morning, and it was not the ancients living in the ruins and shadows, not the splintery specters in the walls that had snared me. It had been my own parents.

It was so dark that I didn't see the flagstone street turn abruptly to wooden planks. I tripped and rolled to a halt, raising a cloud of dust. I rubbed my eyes, and saw a sliver of light in the blackness before me. The light swelled and leaked outward to reveal a door. I heard laughter—sweet, youthful laughter.

I wiped my face and stood. With every step I took towards the door, there was a fluttering modulation in that laughter. I touched the door, pushing it open enough to see that the light was not so bright, that this room was indeed as dilapidated as I should have guessed from the exterior. But now I was sure it wasn't a child's laugh after all.

Whatever furnishings had once filled this room were now no more than a dust-gray spiral of debris—as though chairs, tables and draperies had been shattered in a whirlwind. It looked as if that tempest could reawaken at any moment, so I stepped around the debris, sticking close to the walls. The laughter diminished to a soft, luring tease.

As I rounded the corner I saw the backside of a woman's dress: a pink floral print against faded blue, complemented by tiny bloodstains, the material wrinkling and writhing with her movements. Her arms were flailing at the wall, but I could not see her hands, which disappeared into the shadowy surface.

She was no longer laughing. She was crying, screaming horrible oaths to a person or thing I couldn't quite distinguish from the wood patterns. It was only when I saw the wood grain move and a piece of it reach around her that I realized that the wall—or at least a part of it—was alive, as alive as she or I was. I thought of the little girl sandwiched between those two clutching pieces of wall and the way the wood had breathed apart and then smacked back together again, pinning her into place and enveloping her without ever crushing her.

I was too mesmerized by the kaleidoscopic dance of the wood grain to move or even make a sound. I watched as a great arm of wood rose between the woman's legs and would have pulled her into the wall cavity if the arm hadn't crumbled into slivers and smoke when she squeezed her thighs around it. And then both she and the wall emitted a low, gurgling laugh. A mass of wood rose from the peak of the wall fissure and a face, as craggy as the bark of a tree, turned in my direction and its eyes, as beautiful a blue as my mother's, opened and looked down at me.

And with that, the wall fell silent, and the woman was released from its grip. She whirled around and glared at me with those same eyes, and while a smile spread across the wooden face above her, her own face contorted in anger.

"Spying little bastard!" She staggered towards me, her bloody dress and skin pierced and torn by knifelike splinters. The wall shuddered, its face folded into itself and within moments it was a smooth, lifeless surface. By that time the old woman was almost upon me. "I know who you are, you spying little bastard!"

I turned and sprinted for the door. She laughed, and as if on cue, the entire house and even the doorway through which I dove laughed as well.

I rolled into the avenue. The wood was not so old and gray and crumbling anymore, and it was no longer so dark.

The woman leaned in the doorway. There was no blood on her dress or on her face. She was old, but there was a grandmotherly glow in her features now and a sweetness in her smile unlike anything I thought I would ever see on my parents' faces again.

"Joey Gilliland! Come here and have some fresh-baked brownies, you little sweetheart." I could even smell the brownies. I wanted, needed so badly to believe that if I followed this nice old woman back through the doorway, she would sit me at a table and feed me brownies and milk and tell me stories about my mother that would be so funny I'd laugh milk through my nose.

Instead I ran. No longer towards or away from the light, because the light was everywhere now, a dim but consistent illumination that revealed nothing. In the center of the courtyard was the tree, not so gigantic or warm and inviting as it had once seemed. It served only to obstruct the sunlight that would have otherwise leaked through the dull brown glass ceiling. Besides, there was a crowd surrounding the tree and I wanted no part of crowds. I made my way towards the little house in which I'd lived all summer, not because I had any wish to see my parents, not because I believe they could protect me from or cure me of anything I might encounter in any dark avenue. I wanted only to get a ride with them out of this horrible place, back to a world I barely remembered.

But our little house was dark, and the suitcases my parents had placed just inside the doorway were gone. I ran back to the courtyard, calling out to my mother and father. A few in that crowd turned to look at me and I noticed that there were at least a few children left. I heard a woman screaming, shouting curses I couldn't understand. Some of the crowd laughed, a few shouted back at her, but most turned away, embarrassed. As the crowd began to disperse, the children were jerked away. One of them was the little girl I'd tried to pull from that hungry wedge between the walls, her face swollen and still a little scabby. I called out to her but her father yanked at her arm and escorted her away as she cried in protest. I stood at the edge of the crowd and let them file past me, none dating to meet my eyes except for my cousin Vincent, a look of loathsome satisfaction on his face ... .

And then there were only the five of us. My mother, still shouting at the retreating crowd, so choked by her own tears that I couldn't understand a word she said. That gray, angry old man, still leaning on a cane and staring at his own knuckles. Next to him stood the giant who'd saved the little girl. He was glowering at the final figure in that tableau: a pale, ragged man kneeling on the floor, his tussled hair almost touching the pool of blood and vomit that spread outward from his knees.

My father. At first he seemed not much bigger than me, and so weighted down that he would never be able to unfold himself, never stand upright, never walk away. Never escape the grip that man's stare had on him.

No one would look at the old giant—not my mother, not

the man next to him, and of course not my father. Only me. I could not look away from those glittering blue eyes, the wing-like sweep of white hair across those brow ridges, cheeks so ancient, their lines so deep they resembled the bark on the tree next to him. And that deep, diagonal gash across his face, not so much a scar as a fissure from which he hurled his contempt at my father.

When he turned his gaze toward me, his expression softened, his lips parting into something that may have been meant as a smile.

My father was on his feet when I turned to him again. My mother was quiet, trying to walk alongside him, but she held back when he refused to acknowledge her. He stooped to pick up a pair of suitcases while my mother took the third. Neither spared a look for me. Only the old giant—and now his companion—had eyes for me. I unleashed my most fearsome four-year-old's scowl, then gave a tentative glance to the pool my father had left behind, and then began following my parents towards the set of double doors that led from the Hive to the outside.

Doors I had not seen opened all summer.

There were moments when he seemed to have no idea where the door was, or what was straight ahead, or up, or down. My mother rushed on ahead of him to open the door. As she propped the door open with her suitcase, she saw me as though for the first time, and motioned for me to hurry.

I ran out onto the Hive's dilapidated porch but stopped dead when I saw the clouds drifting across the gray sky, the forest blanketing the horizon, and the sickly translucence of my father's skin as he dropped the suitcases and fell to his knees, sobbing in humiliation. He looked up, meaning to shout something at my mother, but saw me first. He looked so sad and alone. I could not imagine what they had done to him, or why. It was only by living my summer in that Hive, and seeing the expression on that old giant's face, that I could believe the world capable of shaming my father into such a state. His expression spanned so wildly that I thought it was the wind, battering his features about in a cruel game, just for their amusement. Or perhaps for my amusement. *Look, there he is again. Let's see if we can make him laugh!*

Father grabbed my wrist and pulled me to him, hugging me desperately, while my mother called out his name, my name. Our name.

He smelled terrible. Protruding from the side of his neck was a bloody, thumb-sized splinter.

RADIO GLOSSOLALIA

It had nothing to do with the world outside his apartment or the darkness beyond the borders of his reading lamp. It wasn't the irritation or disillusionment he was beginning to feel over the promotional package he was putting together for a film entitled 'Your Urinary System and You' (third edition). And in the end, it wasn't even the realization that he was beginning to detest every piece of music he encountered along the radio dial. He stopped *there*, he dropped everything from his lap, he turned up the volume and just sat there, mouth open and brow tensed, because of what it *was*, all the things it could not be mistaken for, because somewhere deeper than he'd ever known, it was possible to reach inside of himself, he recognized it.

For just an instant Eddie mistook it for a late night evangelist's sermon. There was something to the resonance and cadences of that voice that made him think of the scornful, embittered religious services of his youth. But it wasn't a language he recognized. In fact, it resembled nothing he'd ever heard in his life. The mixture of quick, clipped, and then long, rolling phonemes, and the strange inevitability with which they succeeded each other, seemed almost to hypnotize him. At times the long tones followed one after another, each one sustaining longer than the last, and the voice began to swell into an almost unbearable drone. Occasionally a weak, timid chorus would reply during a pause, or would synchronize with a long, complex passage. Sometimes it fell silent altogether. But it always returned.

For over an hour he sat, concentrating on this chanting, sometimes waiting for it to end so that an announcer would come on and explain what it was, sometimes trying to guess the language, but most of the time just lost within the rhythms and timbres of that Voice, watching as the light around him intensified and the darkness beyond it deepened, and feeling the forms and odors and ideas awaken and squirm in the pit of his being—not ready to rise into his thoughts just yet, but reminding his blood and muscles and bones of their existence.

Eventually the static ate its way through the signal and no amount of fiddling with the dial could bring it back. He sat there for a while, lost, while the room around him came back to life and the vague, primeval hum inside of him faded to silence.

It wasn't until three days later that he even recalled the incident. He couldn't remember where on the radio dial he'd even found it. A vague recognition of the hypnotic excitement those sounds had stirred in him resurfaced, but he dismissed it and moved on to more immediate matters, such as the classroom guide for the video version of 'The Story of the Spleen.'

He found it again, under almost identical circumstances, a month later. It was the same voice, the same ... words. He wondered if it might be a rebroadcast of some kind of avant-garde performance. He decided to wait until its conclusion and find out just exactly what it was, and then remembered how elusive and irretrievable the signal had grown the last time.

He popped a tape into the cassette deck and began recording. He wrote down the frequency at the top of the page on which he was composing his text and then sat back to listen.

It was so irritating, so monotonous, that at first he wondered what had drawn him into it so completely the first time. He turned down the volume and got back to work. But even then, even at a whisper, the Voice was persistent. And it was speaking to him. Eventually the legal pad and his Xeroxed notes were pushed aside and he raised the volume ... and then raised it again. Finally, he fell back into his chair and the world beyond his lamplight receded into an unfocused distance.

The sound of the tape clicking off jolted him out of those weightless, limitless distances. The signal remained strong and clear and the fury of the Voice was intensifying. He flipped the tape over, hit record and sat back pensively, shutting his eyes, trying to recreate a state that had enveloped him only a minute before but which now seemed to have dissipated entirely. The spell was broken.

As a last, desperate resort, he shut off the light.

Where did the black world of his living room, the radio and the Voice end, and where did sleep, with its strange, disturbing dreams begin?

Eddie sat up in the chair at 6:30 AM, looked about the room and listened to the sounds of early morning outside his windows. Inside his head he grabbed at a vocabulary and an encyclopedia of visions that slithered into his unconscious while he was in the very act of trying to recall them. They just … disappeared.

Down there.

There was nothing but static at that frequency on the FM dial. He popped out the tape and grimaced when he realized that he'd just erased his all-time favorite jazz tape: Coltrane's 'A Love Supreme' and Miles Davis' 'In a Silent Way' for the sake of … what?

Something that …

For just a moment something seemed to tug at him: a whisper, an aspect to this room he'd never noticed before. It disappeared with an urgent crack. Reality asserted itself; he looked down at the tape label one last time before peeling it off and tossing the tape into his briefcase.

That morning he gave the tape to Claire, the company's International Marketing Manager, and asked her to listen to it at her leisure, find out what language it was, if she could, and figure out what it all meant.

She had it back that afternoon. She had this look on her face when she handed it back to him, and at first he took it as a sign of recognition.

"What is it? Any idea?"

"Well, it isn't any language I know. It doesn't really sound like a language at all. It's like … glossolalia."

"What?"

"Glossolalia. Speaking in tongues. You know … like a kind of ecstatic prattle …"

He nodded. The expression on her face was severe and … suspicious.

"Eddie? Are you all right? What's this all about?"

"What do you mean?"

"I mean, why'd you do it? And then ask me to tell you what language it was in. Did you really think you were—"

"Wait a second. Do you think that's *me*? I recorded that off the radio. Off of … um … look, 94.5 FM."

"It's *your* voice, Eddie. It's *you*. Don't tell me you got it off the radio. Is this some kind of prank or something?"

He stood suddenly. "Some kind of *prank?*" He could feel the rage tightening his face.

As Claire backed out of his office, he noted a look of fear, even revulsion, in her eyes. He paced the tiny office, trying to think through what had just happened. Finally, he packed up and left, even though it was only 3:15.

When he got home he made a brief recording of his voice and played it back. Then he listened to the tape he'd made the night before.

It *was* his voice. How could he have not recognized his own voice? He listened to every syllable, every shout and whisper, and heard himself. Even the weak background voices sounded like him. He shut it off. He pulled the loop of tape out and began disemboweling it into the trash bin, shouting and swearing as the thin strands of recording tape began to accumulate atop the food scraps and crumpled paper, until the things escaping his mouth no longer sounded like words, and the unwinding vision beneath him ceased to resemble a trash bin full of cassette tape. The tape was alive and squirming with fear as it plunged down the infinite depths of a thorned, segmented gullet, screaming an agonized, pleading reply to the seething stream of glossolalia from Eddie's clenched, frothing mouth.

He stopped, dead silent, and backed away.

That was it. No more! This had to stop, and it *would* stop. *Now.*

When he dared to open his mouth again and speak, he recognized the words as, "There, are we all right now?" He looked into the trash bin. Just trash: food, paper and an unraveled cassette.

He stopped listening to the radio after that. He'd play tapes at night, or just let the TV murmur in the background. Once, however, he did check out 94.5 FM. Nothing but static.

Eddie realized that, whatever had happened on these two, no, *three* occasions, he'd been on the brink of something catastrophic—a breakdown without precedent. He backed off, embraced routine, embraced boredom. He severed what limited, tenuous social contact he had with the outside world. He focused all of his strength on preparing the guides and promotions for an endless, numbing string of educational films and videos.

But even these precautions seemed inadequate. Because nothing was harder to secure than silence and light. The world was a cacophony of voices and machines and music, even the weather had a voice. The most he could hope for was to shut out that cacophony, and even then it was all there—an inviting hum just beyond his windows. And amid all the sunlight and room light there were always shadows, some of them pure black slivers in which anything could appear, leaking out towards the edges of the light, threatening to swallow the world.

But the fears and suspicions appeared ungrounded, and after a few weeks, the brief, flickering movements in the darkness disappeared and he no longer feared, no longer thought about the Voice.

Once again, the real world asserted itself, and he felt its reassuring grip over him, over the sights and sounds that homed in on his eyes and ears. And so he was left friendless and isolated, enmeshed in the minutiae of a job he detested.

And then, one night the following winter, while passing through the nearly deserted tunnel that connected the Dearborn to the State Street subways, there was a blind black man in tattered winter wear, beating out a rhythm with his cup of coins and singing a wordless, blue-noted lament. The glossolalia episode was no more than a harmless memory now, like a long-ago bout of pneumonia, and he hadn't thought about it in some time. Now he stopped and listened to the rich, gravely voice echo down the tiled walls of the tunnel, carefully trying to connect each and every phoneme, to either make out the words or else ... what?

The man quieted down and nodded a greeting at Eddie. Embarrassed that he'd been noticed, he stepped forward, grabbing at the loose change in his pocket as the singing resumed. And as he heard the coins crash and the voice twisting in rhythm to it, a certain, almost recognizable succession of phonemes passes. Chilled, he backed away.

He listened to the singer's echo all the rest of the way down the tunnel, and that vague recognition passed. He reminded himself how nice it was to use this shortcut late at night, away from the crowds, away from the Singing Troll, the obnoxious folksinger who seemed to roost there during every morning and evening rush hour.

Later, while listening to a radio broadcast of the Hindemith Violin Concerto, he began to notice a mumbling static building up from underneath. He tried to readjust the dial but no matter what he did, the interference grew stronger, until finally it overwhelmed and obliterated the music, replacing it with a voice, not his own, but similar to the voice of the blind singer, crying out an ecstatic chant. He turned the dial to a nearby rock station, but within minutes, the glossolalia totally overwhelmed it.

He shut off the radio.

From that point on, the glossolalia asserted its grip on reality just as he'd feared it might the summer before—a whisper or a crackle or a roar that could appear at any time from any source—from a radio, from a passing siren, from the voice of a colleague or television personality, or even the leafless, frozen trees above him. During daylight hours, out in public, the Voice never lasted more than a few seconds, but it was always distinct and unmistakable. At night, in solitude, it was continuous and impossible to escape.

Soon he surrendered himself to the nightly attack. The glossolalia followed him across the radio dial, and he continued to lead it, never trying to escape, just testing the limits of its power over him. It was overwhelming in its persistence.

And yet ... something was missing. He'd concentrate on the nightly broadcasts, stop beneath the whispering trees, eavesdrop on subway conversations that suddenly seemed to degenerate—apparently without anyone else noticing it—into that familiar pattern of sounds. As the winter progressed, he grew fascinated with the way it seemed to be eating away at the world. But it did not have the hypnotic, hallucinogenic effect it had once had on him.

One night, as he was laying in bed in the dark, listening to the Voice, his thoughts retreated to the previous summer, to the vision within the trash bin, and realized that this memory, once so fearful, had suddenly become a source of great yearning. The screams of that unwinding strand of tape had been something more than fear. He recognized that the unseen depths within that pit were the focus of this intense but apparently unquenchable yearning.

He had been opened up for just a few shadowy moments to something vast and monstrous coiled in his core, something that had threatened to explode forth into an all-consuming landscape and population—the reflection of a million years of fear and horror, all filtered through him. The glossolalia was the key to that world. That key burned in his hands and he'd fled from it, afraid to think that he might have to confront and flee from it again.

But all that was changed now. The world itself was now the interference pattern, an overwhelming barrage of visual and aural clutter that had been drowning out the glossolalia for his entire life. And now, nothing more than a withdrawn madman, he could only listen as the glossolalia leaked through the conversations and clattering and hissing that filled his ears, indecipherable descriptions of a world he was too blind to see.

One morning he left the apartment and heard the Voice somewhere above him. It moved through the trees over his head and he could hear, underpinning the whispered chanting, the rustling of cold, bare branches. It teased him like this every morning.

But today, as he crossed the street, the Voice deepened into a roar. He whirled around and saw, peering from that corner tree, the face of a creature formed from the twisted, intertwining branches, its red eyes and mouth gaping, its knotted arms thrashing against the branches. The arms reached out to him ...

There was a screech. He whirled again and saw a car bearing down on him, skidding into a diagonal. He jumped out of the way, landing along the curb. When he looked up he was no more than a few feet from the driver's window. The driver thrust his head out—his face contorted and purple with rage— and began screaming at him. And the Voice ...

He stood slowly, his face blank as the glossolalia poured out of the wrinkled, thorny plates of flesh that extended from the crackling trunk that had once been a neck. The mouth blossomed red and filled his entire field of vision for just an instant and the deafening Voice poured out of the glistening concentric rings that seemed to extend for miles into the depths of that cavity. The mouth snapped shut and he caught a glimpse of the man's "real" face as the car sped away.

He looked around, eyes wide and ears sensitive to every facet of the city-drone filling the air. Everything was normal. There was no tree creature, no chanting, and when he opened his mouth, the only word that emerged was a long, quavering "Shit!"

But the girl in the seat next to him on the train had on a cheap pair of headphones and it was easy to make out the chants that hissed out of her ears. It seemed to have no effect on her, but as he listened, he looked out the window, down at the girders that formed the skeletal structure that elevated the train, and at the darkness beneath them and at the huge, glistening forms that swam down there, some of them looking up with disproportionately small, cold faces.

He shut his eyes, afraid, embarrassed. He opened them just in time to see the train descend into the dark tunnels, which roared back at him in long, slow, deep tones. He was going home. He didn't know what to do. He looked up at all the impassive, silent faces.

Couldn't they hear? Didn't they know? What were they doing here, anyway?

He got off at Jackson and took the stairs down to the tunnel leading to the State Street trains and once again, the chanting filled his ears. The jostling crowds muttered it; the blind man with the clanging cup transformed it into a deep, resonant, melodic song.

The echoing tiles twisted and smiled and sweat.

No one seemed to notice; no one seemed the least bit surprised by the sounds emerging from their mouths. In their coats, their suits, their dresses, with their straight backs and impassive faces, they seemed diminished by their own Voices, by the shivering and breathing of the wall tiles.

The blind man screamed from within the shimmering infestations of his rags, with no face except for a huge, snaggle-toothed mouth. The cup in his hand sang harmony, its own silver mouth curling and smirking at the passing crowd.

He moved on. The people around him were no more than phantoms, slowly withering away around him. He was going home.

But what was this?

It was the pudgy folksinger who seemed to be there every morning and evening rush hour, the singer he referred to as the Singing Troll. He was rasping out some old Jim Croce song, accompanying himself with perfunctory chunks of harmony on an out-of-tune guitar.

The glossolalia that had been resonating, encompassing and reshaping the entire world, suddenly collapsed under this heartfelt whining and strumming. He stopped directly in front of the Singing Troll.

He felt nudges and gusts of warm air as the crowd of phantoms passed through him. But the longer he stood there, the more solid they became, until they began shoving him and yelling at him. The tiles were settled, flat and dry.

"*Shut up!*" he screamed at the Singing Troll.

The man glanced in his direction for just an instant, just a little disturbed, perhaps, but more concerned about not missing a line or a chord change.

He took a step towards the folksinger and bumped into the guy's guitar case. He began to mutter, to speak, to growl. The Voice came spilling out. He screamed into the folksinger's face until the man stopped singing, blinked, and began backing down the wall.

Eddie cut him off and grabbed the guitar out of his hand. He took a broad swing with it, and the body of the guitar crashed against the folksinger's head. The second blow broke through the back of the guitar's body. The fourth blow, which caught him as he was slithering to the floor, shattered the guitar's body altogether. He pounded on the whimpering, curled-up form on the floor with the neck of the guitar.

This last vestige, this intrusive, fleshy, raspy voiced chunk of interference began to spread across the floor, a thick stew of blood, corduroy, and fat, while slithering things began to rise through that stew, singing out in wordless liberation.

He tossed away the splintered neck. The tunnel was empty. The glossolalia was deafening. The tunnel undulated, pulling him forward on peristaltic waves, so he moved on, as the tiles buckled and breathed. The roaring emerged from the walls— from the scales that had once been tiles, from the breathing spaces between them, but especially from the vast, flickering pit towards which he was now headed.

Ages passed and his walk had weakened into off-balanced staggering, when the chanting quieted to a hush and a hunched figure appeared on the floor ahead of him. He was layered in rages and gave off an overwhelming stench. Eddie stepped in front of this mound of festering rags, saw the one crooked, skeletal leg twisting out from underneath and watched as the blue, folded mound of flesh at the rag mound's peak swelled and lifted and something like a face looked up at him.

Its eyes were bulging and blind white, its nose was a jagged-lipped cavern at the center of its face, and its upper jaw was a long, tusked ridge. Underneath it, two lower jaws danced gracefully as they locked alternately in and out of position beneath that ridge. Each lower jaw was twisted and toothless, and each had its own serpentine tongue. It was the dance of these tongues and the steady outpouring of air from that flesh-fringed hole of a nose that generated the chant, now little more than a whisper. It was beautiful, full of things longer and shorter and far more potent and ancient than … words.

. The face looked at him. He recognized his own face in there somewhere, and recognized the entreaty. He began to chant along. The walls were lined with faces that had once been scales that had once been tiles. They too were chanting now. An ooze spread across the floor, flowing ahead and downward into a watery depth where a thousand long-necked, short-necked, no-necked faces protruded from the ceiling, the walls, the bubbling liquid floor. But of course this cramped, slithering, screaming morass into which he now stepped was not a confinement, it was an opening, it was the real, external world now, unbounded and with room for an infinite number of faces, an infinite number of voices ...

... and all the faces and all the voices were his and all spoke the simple, unfathomable, and inescapable truth, and that truth was that all the faces and all the voices were his and all spoke the simple, unfathomable, and inescapable truth, and that truth was...

SNOWLIGHT

My father was dead. Freshly dead. My family was reeling with an unpalatable and unpredictable mixture of shock, grief, and resentment. More and more I tried to keep away from them, just as more and more of them kept piling off of planes and trains and I began to realize just what a big, monstrous brood my family really was. Relatives who remembered me only as a baby—if at all—were suddenly scrutinizing me, correcting me, reproaching me and just measuring me all the way around, wondering how this scrawny, sullen twelve-year-old was going to be anything but a hindrance to his poor, grief-stricken mother.

Beyond that, my father's death was something that officially had very little to do with me. It was talked about all the time in my presence, but I never entered into these talks. His death, my mother's difficult situation, even the problem of... me; it was as though they were speaking a language I wasn't supposed to understand.

And so no one noticed the disease, the cavity opening in my mind—no one except my mother, who in several instances seemed to recognize a malevolence in the emptiness of my eyes. She never did anything about it—didn't talk to me about it, didn't even talk around it. It was as if she refused to acknowledge it.

Within two weeks of my father's death a dozen blackheads erupted on my face, I got my first gray hair, and I had one of my molars shattered in a schoolyard fight. I could feel an ugly momentum building in me, and I saw nothing in my path to hinder its acceleration. The moment I surrendered to it, I realized I actually liked it. Preferred it, in fact.

It was 1967, the winter of the big snow that paralyzed all of Chicagoland and turned the children's world into a vast alien wasteland of snowdrifts and abandoned cars. My friends and I basked in the pain and the glory of the big snow. We shoplifted from the barren stores in the mall, skitched, and pelted houses, cars, and helpless adults with snowballs.

On January 27th, we scaled the drift-slopes at the edge of the mall parking lot up onto a deserted, drift-covered Eisenhower Expressway, where we waved our arms in defiance, smoked Marlboros with the filters broken off, and talked about what we'd do if we caught a car struggling through the drifts.

My own suggestion was to torture and kill the occupants, cook them in the blaze of their ignited automobile, eat them, make jewelry and weapons from their bones, and use the wreckage as a barricade for our next victims. I was just kidding. It was the kind of thing a kid like me, with my reading and TV habits, would consider a joke. But my friends, constantly reveling in their fantasies of sex, vandalism, and street-fighting, were appalled by my suggestion and let me know it in no uncertain terms.

Normally I'd have been considered far too weird to be part of that gang, though I'd been moving along its fringes for the last year or so. But lately my stock seemed to have risen considerably. I was morbid, I was ferocious, I hated almost everybody, and my whole bell jar childhood of comic books and science fiction films had just crumbled around me, leaving behind something nervous and desperate and doomed to explode at any moment. They let me tag along because they wanted to be there when I finally went off. They kicked me around, and yet... somehow, just as my mother was, they were afraid of me. They knew that sooner or later, I'd do something.

As I surely would have, sooner or later...

That weekend three of us had been hauled in for skitching on the back of an unmarked police car. I was supposed to be grounded for the next five weeks. On Tuesday night I found out that my brother and sister and their families, plus a few of my least favorite aunts and uncles were all coming over for the evening. I balked. I went hysterical and stormed out of the house. There was no way I was going to spend an entire evening listening to them lecture me on the importance of not mumbling and above all having good eye contact when I talked to people.

So I hooked up with Bob Ritchie and Jimmy Bugella over on the corner by Jimmy's house. They were going to go smoke cigarettes in an unoccupied house Jimmy's brother had recently broken into. I was far too jittery for that and said so, suggesting that we go up on the ridge over O'Neill Road and pulverize passing cars with snowballs.

Bob groaned and spit into the snow at my feet. "Man, we've been snowballing cars since first grade and we're getting pretty fucking sick of it. Besides, you can get in more trouble if you're caught breaking into a house than you can throwing snowballs at cars."

"Come on, Pickett, my brother says the place is really safe."

So I was pushed and badgered into going to the abandoned house. It was fairly remote, set far back from the road and surrounded by trees. From the outside it looked perfectly normal. In the months to follow, the interior and finally the exterior of that house would be trashed, and a week before the end of the school year it would be burnt to the ground. As we approached we could hear yelling and crashing coming from inside.

We saw Larry Lorazo out front. He told us that Jimmy's brother was in there with two of his friends, and they were arguing with two big greasers from the Cozy Club. He told us it wouldn't be too cool to go in there and Bob and Jimmy agreed. We stood around, listening to the five of them screaming at each other while we smoked Chesterfields from a pack Larry had stolen from his mom.

"Let's snowball cars," I muttered under my breath, just trying to annoy them.

"Yeah, man," Larry beamed, "Let's do it! I'd love to nail my stepfather's car with iceballs, drive the son of a bitch off the road and—BAM! Into a fuckin' tree! Let's do it!"

Bob and Jimmy grunted and mumbled, looked back at the house but made no move one way or another. We just smoked and listened to the escalating noise inside.

"Those Cozys sound really pissed off," Bob whispered. "Shouldn't we do something?"

"What? Call the cops?"

"Naaah. Hey man, I'm just thinking about your brother."

"Fuck my brother! I hope they shoot the jagoff!"

They all laughed. Had I thought Jimmy really meant it, I might have laughed, too.

Time for my refrain: "Let's snowball cars!"

There was a unanimous cry as we trudged off through the snow. Every step was an effort as we pulled our legs out of one drift only to plunge into another, never knowing when we'd sink up to our waists into some inconspicuous snow trap. I just tagged along behind, listening to every stupid remark, smoking twice as many cigarettes as any of them, and thinking about all my relatives in my mom's living room, everyone bad-mouthing me, and her just listening and nodding, and I wondered, was she thinking of me now? Did she wonder, imagine, worry where I might be?

I coughed up a gob and flicked my cigarette into the snow. Besides these escapades with my friends, what did I really have to live for? You look at the emptiness, the madness, at the circumstances that seem inevitable in your life, and it frightens and sickens you, watching it from the outside like that. And then one day you realize that it doesn't bother you the way it once did and that it's no longer some dreaded inevitability. It's become the routine, and the horror has instead become a kind of emptiness. My own emptiness refueled me now, and I refilled that emptiness with my rage, and thus filled, found for myself a nice, quiet equilibrium. I could die now, I thought. I could die and just...not be anymore...and not fret, not cry or worry about it. There was nothing but the edge—whatever edge I could grope up to, and then, the easy business of being dead afterwards.

Charlie Frantantian (a kid we all hated because his older brother Rick had beat up Bob's big sister and raped her back when we were in kindergarten) lived in a house with a side yard that edged right out to a peak that stood about ten feet over O'Neill Road. There was a large maple tree there, roots exposed by erosion along the edge of the road. It was a perfect place to set up our firing nest, with good visibility and plenty of cover, far enough from the Frantantian house that we could smoke and yell all we wanted without getting the cops called on us. As for Charlie Frantantian, he was the toughest kid in the seventh grade, as well as the oldest, but he didn't have many friends, and the four of us as a group—especially with Jimmy Bugella, who was possibly the third or fourth toughest kid in the seventh grade—were more than a match for him.

It was obvious why Bob and Jimmy were so weary of nailing cars like this. It was possibly the world's best vantage point for this kind of game, and it was just too easy to get a good shot or get away if someone had the urge to come after us. It was a busy one-way street without another side street to turn on for almost a quarter mile. And the truth was that there was just too much snow. Too many drifts and too many new snowfalls. People trudged through snow, drove through it, and lately were even growing immune to being pelted with it.

So it became a matter of temperament. Larry Lorazo could easily imagine that every car was his stepfather's and get fresh satisfaction out of every projectile thumping against the hood or exploding across the windshield. And I could pretend it was... who? My hatred was too congested and all too much a thing, an obstruction in itself. It was every snowball I threw, just as it was every car I hit and, to an even more extreme degree, it was every car I missed.

But Bob Ritchie and Jimmy Bugella were already real hoods whose role models were their tough brothers in high school. Throwing snowballs at cars was just too petty and childish a way of causing trouble, not when you could bust a kid up, break his parents' windows, spray paint their...well, anything, steal stuff bigger than what you could just slip easily into your pockets, cop feels from girls in your class and persist until one day one of them spread her legs for you....

In the vast scheme of things, snowballing cars was just short of nothing.

The highlight was a station wagon with ten little kids and

two grandparenty types in the front seat. The four of us must have hit it at least a dozen times. When the guy tried slamming on his brakes he began to spin out, thought better of it, and kept going.

I let loose my last snowball.

"Aww, man, see the way I nailed his license plate?" I cried.

"Pickett, you fucking palsy!" Larry growled. "I hit that plate!"

Larry Lorazo was about my height, about ten pounds heavier than me; a kid who'd given me a lot of grief back in third, fourth grades. We both remembered that, even though we tolerated each other reasonably well because we hung out with most of the same guys. But Larry still made occasional attempts to assert his place above me in the pecking order. This was just one more example. He'd let loose his last snowball before the station wagon had begun to spin, and we all knew it.

It wasn't a matter of pride. It wasn't even me retargeting my anger. I don't know why I hit him. It stunned everyone so much that I managed to hit him twice more, a second time in the nose and then in the rib cage, before anyone said or did a thing. Larry punched me and elbowed me in the face before I got to him again, kneeing him in the face, throwing him down and sitting on his chest, feeding him snow.

I was pulled off and thrown to the ground as Jimmy and Bob picked him up and walked him away, trying to calm him. When they neared the curb I could hear Larry screaming how he'd "Kill the fucker!" with Bob and Jimmy talking away, too quiet for me to hear. Whatever they were saying to him was calming him down. The three of them continued to talk for a while, and I began to hear sobbing. And then, Larry's broken voice rising again: "I'll kill the fucker!" I stepped away from the tree, trying to catch their words without letting them see me, and suddenly realized that I wasn't the fucker. Not at all. Not anymore. It was his stepfather. And I could hear the consoling tones in their voices as they talked to him, and I remembered those first few days after my dad died, and the stern, protective air they had towards me.

When they came back, Larry wasn't with them.

"Way to go, Pickett. Beatin' up one of your own, for no reason."

"Hey, what do you mean? You hear what he called me? I hit that license plate. I..."

"So what?" Jimmy snapped. "Jesus, you are a fucking palsy! So you pick out someone you know you can take, and you beat him up just 'cause he called you a fucking name. You asshole. You been acting like a jerk ever since your old man died!"

"Larry's old man beat him up tonight. And then he gets punched out by a scrawny shit like you!" Bob flicked a still-smoldering cigarette butt at my jacket. It bounced off and hissed a tunnel through the snow.

"We've known Larry since second grade, man. Who the hell were you back then? What makes you think we want you with us here? Huh?"

They took my cigarettes, lit up, and decided to nail a few more cars. I sat about ten feet away, listening as they got into the rhythm of the game. They stopped talking about me, about Larry and his old man, and just talked about the kinds of cars they were hitting. I was amazed at how much they could find to say about each one, at how clever their remarks seemed. I had grown up one of the good kids, the smart kids, and yet, in every sense that seemed to count anymore, these two proto-greasers outclassed me. Nothing I was or had ever wanted to be stood for anything anymore.

I didn't dare walk over and join them, afraid I was going to start crying.

Larry had cried, there at the edge of Frantantian's driveway, but that was different. There was no way I was going to let that happen to me, not over something as meager and unjustifiable as my own shame. After all, I was the guy who had yet to cry even once about my own dad, after a whole month.

I wondered if anyone had brought that up back at my house. "Hey, Pickett! You're missing all the theater traffic, man!"

I sulked over. Jimmy turned and smiled his toothy, threatening grin, as though nothing had happened. He tossed a snowball at me. I caught it, kneeled into the drift, watching the rows of headlights rolling towards us.

The people were fairly unresponsive. Occasionally someone would honk at us. As the traffic thickened it slowed down and we had to be more and more careful about revealing ourselves. Bob and Jimmy got into an argument over what were the best songs on the radio during the school year so far. Bob held out for '96 Tears' by ? and the Mysterians, 'You Can't Hurry Love' by the Supremes, and 'Psychotic Reaction' by the Count Five.

"Oh yeah? What about 'Ruby Tuesday'? What about 'Eleanor Rigby'? 'Devil with the Blue Dress On'? Come on, Pickett, help me out here."

I wondered if I had a voice left. "All the good songs came out last summer," I grumbled. "There won't be as many good songs all school year as there were last summer. Think about it. 'Hanky Panky, ' 'Summer in the City, ' 'Along Comes Mary, ' 'Paint it Black,' 'Wouldn't It Be Nice'..."

"'They're Coming to Take Me Away'!"

"'Over, Under, Sideways, Down'!"

"'Lady Jane'!"

"'Good Lovin''!"

"Naaa, that came out last spring. How about 'Hey Joe'?"

"And 'Hey Little Girl'?"

"'Wild Thing'!"

"'DIRTY WATER'!"

"Shit," Bob said in amazement. "You're right. I'd never even thought about it. Last summer was the best. It ain't ever gonna get that good again. Not now. Not with the Monkees it ain't."

"Yeah, now we get crap like Winchester Cathedral.' 'Snoopy and the Red Baron.'

"'Mellow Yellow'..."

"'The Eggplant that Ate Chicago'..."

"Aww, hey, man. I like that song!"

"Hey, hey... Oh, shit! Look at this!"

Jimmy pointed down the road. I looked, and a chill ran through me, an unaccountable revulsion as I first set eyes on those headlights, wider apart than any others on the road, moving as though in slow motion, silent and completely isolated from all the other cars.

"Jesus Christ! It's a fuckin' Packard!"

"Bullshit, man. That's a Caddy!"

"Ahh, you don't know shit about cars, Ritchie, ya jagoff."

I let loose a snowball. "I don't care what it is," I cried. "Let's get it!"

We must have hit it ten times before we heard the sound. It had just passed us. It wasn't as though it slammed on its brakes. On this afternoon's fresh slush, those tires would have sent that hulk of metal sailing, even at the slow speed it was moving. It just suddenly...stopped dead, a jolting stop that was coupled with a deep, monstrous hiss.

And then it began to back up, sending traffic skidding and honking. It was backing up towards this street.

"Holy shit," Jimmy cried. "This guy's pissed off!"

By the time we were out from beneath the tree, the car was turning the corner.

We cut a diagonal across the Frantantians' back yard and across the next two yards before we cut over to the street. There was no sign of the car. We ran half a block and only stopped then because of Jimmy's outstretched arms. "Okay," he whispered, "We're all right."

Bob whistled. "Man, that guy was maaad!"

"What the hell was that thing?" I asked. "It didn't look like a Cadillac."

"No way. You know, I think it was a Checker Marathon."

"Whaaa?"

"You know, a cab, but not painted like a cab."

Bob spit. "Naaa, it was too big for that."

"I still say it was a Packard."

"Did you hear that hissing when it stopped? Like it had air brakes."

"Aw, great. Now it's a fucking truck."

Suddenly there was an explosive, metallic roar behind us. We were drowned in a field of yellow light.

We whirled around to see the car bearing down on us. Beams from its twin spotlights slashed at us.

"Split up!" Jimmy cried as he jumped one way, while Bob and I jumped the other way. I slid and fell into the street.

The tire that skidded to a halt only two feet away from

my head was enormous. For an instant I caught my clear but distorted reflection in the hubcap. In the next instant the door was opening and I was on my feet and running up the front lawn of the nearest house. I caught a glimpse of Bob disappearing between two houses on my right.

I slipped into the shadows along the side of the house. The car door was shut and the car was idling. I couldn't see a sign of anybody, in or outside the car. I backed into a metal garbage can, lost my balance, slipped on the ice and fell to the ground, catching my forehead on the twisted metal handle.

I touched the fresh cut near my temple as I stumbled to my knees and crawled behind the row of three trash cans. I huddled there, listening, rubbing my blood between my ungloved fingertips.

Time seemed to freeze. A lifetime passed through me in a single breath. I wondered if I would ever be able to move again.

The spell was broken abruptly by the sound of one of the trash cans being kicked against the brick wall and then sent flying across the snowdrifts at the house next door.

I jumped to my feet. At twelve-and-a-half I must have been all of one inch over five feet tall, so I may be wrong, but facing him for the first time, he seemed to be at least eight feet tall. I could see only his silhouette now but could already feel the monstrous presence in that shadowy face. He lifted the second trash can off the ground.

It wasn't until he held the can high over his head, with paper bags tumbling onto the ice, that I realized what he intended to do.

The sound of that can against the ice was a sickening thud. I wasn't far enough from the impact not to be shaken by its implications. I heard the other can crash and turned back to see him, with his quick but bent and clumsy gait, following me across the yard. I leaped over the fence and landed on hands and knees in the alley. My ungloved right hand slapped down hard, impacting all the way to the gravel.

By the time I got back on my feet he was at the fence. As I ran I heard the fence shatter.

I ran past three houses and then ducked through a backyard,

over a fence and across the street. He was no more than twenty feet behind me the whole time.

And I was moving in the wrong direction. I was now two blocks east of the street where we'd split up, and I was moving farther from my house, from Jimmy and Bob's houses, towards the fringes of town. From here on, the houses were farther and farther apart. Sooner or later they would give way to the quarry and industrial park.

But he was moving too fast and covering too much ground with every step for me to double back. It was almost as though he was funneling me in the direction of his own choice.

I tried to cut around corners every chance I got. Once I managed to get myself turned towards the west as I rounded a garage, but found him standing there, blocking my path. A glint of light hit the face, or that mass of tissue where the face should have been.

A staccato pattern whistled through one of the orifices at the front of the head.

I opened my mouth to scream but nothing came out but a cold, hoarse gasp. I stepped back once, twice, and he didn't move. I took off, sprinting as fast as I could in my constrictive winter wear, out into the drift-white wasteland separating the houses here on the edge of town. Half of my steps deposited me in snow up to my hips.

The first time I looked back I could see his silhouette trudging after me, at what under any other circumstances would have seemed a safe distance—thirty or forty yards. The fact that I saw him at all only convinced me to run faster.

I didn't look back until I was among the trucks along the edge of the quarry, a good half a mile past the last house. I couldn't see any movement and so for a moment wondered if maybe I'd actually shaken him—lost him or tired him or just discouraged him.

And then I thought of that... face. His size. The way he'd brought down that can in a blow that had to have been intended to kill me. I looked around. Was all this a dream?

I felt a throbbing pain in my right palm. I took off my left glove and felt the wet abrasions with my fingertips. I gently flicked away the alley rubble and searched for that right glove. It was gone and I couldn't remember when I'd last had it on.

Somehow I had to find another route home. There was no way I could retrace my steps and so I had the choice of cutting north and moving parallel to the expressway, or continuing south as I seemed to be doing now, along the heavier machinery on the quarry's perimeter. I stood a better chance of finding my way back home if I followed the expressway, but I couldn't bear the thought of getting back on O'Neill Road.

So I continued to move past the heavy machinery, most of which was hidden beneath sweeping, untrampled peaks of snow. And as I walked, and especially as I left the quarry, crossed a road and into the parking lot of the Pohl Company, I felt a chill gnawing at the real world.

It began to snow.

The flakes were big, and dropped in clusters on this windless night. Within a few minutes the snowfall was so thick that I couldn't see where I was going. My only beacons were the lights that stood high over the landscape, softened by the haze of the snow. I became completely disoriented and began to wonder if it was worth it to keep walking at all.

So I sat for a while and examined the abrasions on my palm and forehead. I grew hypnotized by the vast perspectives revealed in the illuminated falling snow, felt myself pulled away from the events that had marred my life all winter. I lay back in a snowdrift, staring up at the sky, blinking the snowflakes away and thinking about my Dad.

I sat up with a start, wondering how long I'd been on the ground like this, unsure of whether I'd fallen asleep or not. I struggled to my feet. Every joint seemed to ache as I took those first few steps, but as I walked the pain slowly subsided. So I had to walk, had to keep moving. A layer of snow was dropping from my coat and pants as I staggered up to a snow-laced chain-link fence.

I no longer knew where I was or what time it was or whether I would ever find my way out of this wasteland. Everything around me, especially the dark, hulking shapes on the other side of the fence, seemed somehow unreal, as though beneath the drifts and the freshly fallen snow lay a world not as I had ever known it, but as the disease within me was recreating it. In fact, everything that had happened to me since we'd first set eyes on that car seemed—not like a dream—but like the doom that pervaded my life and dreams, leaking out and warping the world to suit the madness and bitterness that tainted every aspect of my life.

"Pickett! Hey Danny!" came a hoarse whisper on the other side of the fence. I saw a shape move out from behind one of the giant, snow-draped machines. "Is that you?"

Bob Ritchie. He looked from side to side and then ran up to the fence. "Shit, man! What are you doin' here?"

"That guy followed me! Shit, Bob, I think the guy was trying to kill me."

"Followed you? But… have you seen him?"

"Not for a while. What are you doing out here?"

"Just climb the fence."

'Why don't *you* climb the fence?"

"Shut up and climb. Anyway, I got the fags."

He backed away, disappearing through a wall of falling snow. I made a slow, unsteady ascent up the twelve-foot fence. As I reached the top the entire fence wavered beneath my shaking, weakening arms. I leaned in too hard against the sharp twists at the top, cut my face and ripped my coat. I was afraid to go over the edge. I swallowed hard and looked about me at the transfigured night. I could see the vast space surrounding me, the open fields, the gaping sky, but the air was so thick with snow that I felt enclosed in a small room whose boundaries were a pulsing haze—easy to break through but impossible to escape. I could see no sign of Bob Ritchie.

I lost my balance and then my grip, and fell the twelve feet into the snow bank, my little room still firmly in place around me.

I struggled to my feet, feeling the frustration well through me, that feeling that I could do nothing right. No, it was the feeling that misfortune not only seemed to follow me but actually radiated from me and infected the world around me. I'd killed my father, perpetuated my mother's grief, created all these nasty-tempered drones who called themselves my relatives, and now, finally, created a monster and a snow-smothered wasteland of twisted metal to bring about my death. The Big Snow of 1967 was nothing more than all of my frozen tears, unable to come out any other way.

"What kind of place is this?" I heard a haunted voice and thought I recognized it as my own.

"Ahh, this is just a bunch of old scrap from the Pohl Company. We trashed all this shit years ago." Bob Ritchie emerged from the shadows of a great machine, smoking a cigarette.

"Is he here?" I asked.

"I don't think so. Anyway, why did you say he chased you out here? I mean, the guy was right behind me 'til about ten minutes ago."

"Well, then there's two of 'em, 'cause someone came out of that car after me, and he chased me all the way out here."

"Naaah... There was only one person in that car. A big guy."

"Yeah, a real big guy. I saw his face. Jesus Christ! I mean... he hasn't got a face at all!"

"Shit, he was just some guy. Some drunk, I'll bet. He was probably after both of us and we were so scared we couldn't see each other the whole time. But we shook him. See? Here, have a fag."

I took a cigarette, lit up and gazed at the field of snow. "I don't think so," I coughed as I pointed. "Look."

Over a hundred yards away, beneath the snow-filtered glow of a light, a figure staggered, tall and broad, with arms that hung nearly to his knees. "That's him," I whispered.

"Yeah, okay. You're right. But look, Danny, see how he staggers? Just a drunk. Some old boozer, like Larry's old man."

"He's coming this way."

"He'll never get us. Wait a second." He began digging in the snow at the foot of the machine, finally pulling up a length of steel rod with a twisted, jagged tip. "See, I told you we trashed these things years ago. Here, you take this." He pushed it at me and then dug some more, until he came up with another piece.

"Just in case the guy does catch us, we'll crack him with these. Hell, we'll knock him out and take his money. How's that? You with me?"

I lowered my head. I wanted to believe Bob Ritchie, I wanted to trust his judgment. I needed to trust it. But Bob was wrong. I couldn't feel his fear, but I knew it was there. It had to be.

"Check out the way he walks, Danny. The guy can barely stand. We can take him!"

"The guy who chased me was fast."

"All right! All right! Come on. I know a place we can go. We'll hide in the tunnels."

"Tunnels? No fucking way!"

"Ahhh, come on!" He started and I followed. "They're big pipes of that corrugated sheet metal stuff. They've been here for years. We used to play war in 'em all the time when we were kids."

As we walked I tried to imitate his air of self-assurance, tried to walk as though I was cool and cocky and enjoying myself. All the while I was feeling sick inside, wondering what Bob Ritchie was really thinking.

The tunnels were just as he'd described them. Corrugated sheet metal pipes, anywhere from ten to thirty feet long and almost five feet in diameter. As we approached, we passed concrete blocks from which bouquets of tall, twisted cable grew, spreading into the night skies like electric trees, arching over us like a forest canopy. I could hear a distinct buzzing noise but never had the chance to pinpoint the source.

We ducked into one of the pipes, moved through it, stepped briefly back into the snow and then into another. We sat down and had a smoke. My throat was hurting pretty bad now and I had to suppress the nagging tickle.

I kept my eyes on the barely visible face of Bob Ritchie, trying to read him. I kept my ears to the sounds outside.

"Bob? What kind of car was that?"

"I don't know." His whisper was softer than mine as he spoke, occasionally spitting out a pinched speck of tobacco. "A Hudson Hornet maybe. I bet your brother would know."

I was coughing now, trying to catch and propel a worm of

phlegm from my throat. It wouldn't come, and I couldn't stop coughing, or keep the cough from getting louder. Suddenly Bob clutched my forearm and let out a hiss.

There was a sound nearby. At first I couldn't make it out, but as it passed us, I realized it was someone's hand brushing against the ripples of the metal. Accompanying it was a deep, troubled breathing, in synch with a thin, fluttering whistle. We backed in the other direction, watching the circular opening at the end of the tunnel, and finally, the silhouette of a man staggering against the snowlight. We gasped, pushed against each other for the lead, and ran.

Bob dashed through a maddening labyrinth of those tunnels, almost losing me on several tight turns. When he stumbled and fell inside one of the pipes, I tumbled right over him.

We sat up breathless and cursing.

"This isn't right," I whined. "Nothing about this is right! That guy, this place. It's all wrong. Don't you see? Like I'm in a dream!"

"Shhh! Don't wet yourself, Pickett. Let's just...listen a minute."

The silence was so intense, so strained, and the cough trying to escape me so violent, I was afraid that by letting it out I'd shatter not only the silence but everything around me, leaving only me in black, borderless space. "Okay," he whispered at last. "Let's go."

Suddenly, directly behind his head came a thunderous crash, denting the metal inward. We barely had the chance to react when there was another, in the same spot, tearing open the tunnel. A hand, an arm, burst through so quickly that its fingers were wrapped around Bob's arm before we had a chance to run.

"Hit it! Hit it!" he screamed, his voice more desperate every instant. We beat and beat at that arm with our metal pipes, again and again until it was only me beating it and then even I had to stop because the arm had retreated and Bob, whose screams were dying into a whimpered gurgling, was pulled bloodily through the jagged-toothed tear of metal that was far too small for him.

I ran out of the tunnel and was confronted by another. I couldn't quiet myself now, as I stumbled, slapping my arms against the metal shells, coughing and whimpering with complete abandon, knowing that there was no way I would lose him making all this noise, and knowing that I would never find my way out of this cluster of giant pipes before he caught me. It was too late to hold back, too late to think or control my panic. All the tears smoldering inside me for the last month erupted, and my crying grew louder and louder with every turn.

And then, he stood before me, as if he'd just appeared out of thin air, blocking my path, the pitifully small and broken body of my friend hanging limp in his hand, the snowlight illuminating the front of his head, the grotesque field of flesh where a face should have been but wasn't.

I stopped. The pipe hung loose at my side as I stared at him. Neither of us moved. His hand opened and Bob Ritchie's body fell lifeless into the snow. The front of the giant's head twisted and contorted. The flesh began to pop and peel away in a slashing diagonal down his face, exposing blunt, oversized teeth that gleamed in the light. He laughed a familiar laugh.

And then I knew. Or thought I knew.

"NO!" I howled and tried to bolt. I felt the hand at my shoulder, the hot, death-fouled breath across the back of my neck. I turned with the pipe and caught him across the side of the head — a clean blow, unexpected and unblocked. I could feel the resonance of that connection all through my body.

He was leaning too far forward and the impact sent him sprawling. He fell sideways into the corrugated metal, his hands trying to break the fall. I hit him again, bringing the pipe straight down with both hands and all of my ninety-three pounds, feeling the head give beneath it. He let out a strange cry as his hands flailed —at me, at his split head—I don't know which.

I threw the pipe at him and ran.

My hands and body were wet with blood. My face was awash with tears and the snow melting against my cheeks as I ran. I found my way out of the maze of tunnels and began running through the open fields of snow, no longer caring where I was or where I might end up.

I knew I hadn't stopped him. He wasn't human. And though he was at least two feet taller than my father, he had my father's laugh.

I had no idea where I was when I finally found myself running along the edges of backyards. I moved between two houses and out towards an unfamiliar street. I slipped in the fresh snow and fell flat on my face in the street as a car came skidding around the corner. It slammed on the brakes as I rolled away, and looked up to see a '63 Bonneville full of greasers.

"Stupid little son of a bitch!" one of them growled as they passed, leaning out the passenger window and hurling a beer can that caught me in the cheek.

And then they were gone. The cheek stung. I could smell the beer in my hands as I clutched my face.

As I got up on the sidewalk I heard another car approaching the corner. It was garbage night on this block and the sidewalk was lined with cans, so I ducked behind one and watched as a Corvair came to a stop almost directly in front of me. I thought I recognized the car as one of our neighbors'. I crept out and grabbed the back fender just as he pulled away from the stop sign. It was an easy skitch, sliding along the snow that lay fresh against the ice-impacted street. I sank my head between my arms, smelled the exhaust and watched the street pass beneath me.

When I finally let go of the fender I was only four blocks from my house. I brushed myself off and began the slow trudge home. I thought of Jimmy Bugella, safe at home all this time. How could I explain Bob's death to him—or anyone? Could I even admit to having witnessed it? A boy, one of my best friends, suddenly reduced to a lifeless bag of collapsing, draining tissue, discarded in a snowdrift.

Suddenly I was struck by yellow light, as the giant's car screamed to a halt in front of me. A door opened and slammed and a shape was slapped down on the hood.

I backed away as my eyes adjusted to the light and I saw him clearly. The twisting pattern of teeth widened and parted into what almost seemed to be a hideous smile as he let out a dry, staccato whistle.

I was too exhausted to run. I couldn't even move. I felt his palm atop my head, the fingertips like gouged files pressing against my temples. I dropped to my knees and curled into the slush.

"Don't hurt me," I sobbed, "Please don't hurt me. I'm sorry... I didn't mean it... any of it... I don't wanna die, I don't wanna be dead. Please, please... I'll make it up to you. Father..."

He pulled the hand away. The whistling erupted into laughter. At first I was sure that it was my father's laugh, but as it continued, growing louder and filling the night, I realized that wasn't it at all, and the memory, the recognition it stirred in me was something deeper, more distant. I remembered waking up screaming behind the bars of my crib, seeing my father enter the room, and shuddering at the deep, angry tone of his voice. In that moment and in so many others just like it, the shadowy figure in my dream had fused with the dark side of my father.

He backed away. I heard a thump, then went sprawling into the street-slush as a body was hurled into me, a body which seemed to fall apart on impact. I struggled to get away as its arms flailed powerfully against mine even as they seemed to detach from the body. When I got free and looked down at the limp form on the street, I recognized it immediately.

So it was no surprise when I looked up and found the car had disappeared without a trace. Because Jimmy Bugella had cut off in the other direction—he would have been home before I'd even made it to the quarry. And yet it was his broken, mangled body at my feet.

I screamed, loud enough for anyone within a block's radius to hear me through locked doors and storm windows. I was standing alone and blood soaked over the remains of one of my best friends, and there was no way I could ever have explained how it had happened. And so it occurred to me how this might look to cops, or to those people who'd come in response to my screams.

So I ran. Mom would understand. No... no, maybe she wouldn't, but she'd listen, and believe, and hold me, and I could cry at last and tell her all the things about Dad that I missed but was already losing the ability to remember and express. And then it would be over. She'd protect me, solace me, move me away somewhere where no one would think or suspect that any of this had anything to do with me. Because it didn't, couldn't have anything to do with me, and she'd believe that. Mother, you'll believe just this once that there really are monsters, won't you? And that they exist quite apart from whatever dark and diseased thoughts I may have and you may have noticed in my eyes...

And then I saw the cars. My sister and her family's car, my Aunt Helen and Uncle Frank's station wagon, my Uncle Robert's car and my brother Skip's Austin Healey. I knew what I'd find of the other side of that door. All those people, surrounding and obscuring my mom, their words and features stern and uncomprehending. There was no place to go. And I knew that the bone-splintering reality soaking through me would not merely be unbelievable but inconsequential within the realm of their complex, troubled, so thoroughly adult thoughts.

The five steps up my front porch were the most strenuous steps of the entire night. I thought I was going to vomit on the welcome mat.

No sooner did I pull open the storm door than my sister Jeanine opened the inner door. She grabbed me by the wrist, swiftly found the bare skin under my coat and shirt and dug in with her nails and hissed between grinding teeth: "Where have you been? Do you realize it's 10:30? We were about to call the police on you, you little brat. Mother's worried half to death about you." She let go as we left the hallway shadows and entered the living room light.

And there they were, all talking at once, to me, to each other, who knows? I missed most of it. My mom's brother Robert, the eccentric sixty-year-old fascist bachelor, sitting straight-backed in his chair, looking at me from under sweeping white eyebrows that looked like bird wings. My dad's sister Helen and her husband Frank, both drunk out of their minds, their voices booming above the rest. Jeanine's husband Ronnie, looking for all the world like Dennis the Menace's dad, trying to look concerned but beneath it all bored out of his mind just to be enduring yet another evening with all these people. My brother Skip, smiling, popping gum, quiet and trying to look friendly and sympathetic. His bride Donna, who was talking to the small, shadowy figure in the far corner—my mom, answering Donna in hushed tones and looking at me in a way she'd looked at Dad a thousand times, with cold, unredeemable contempt.

The droning in my ears subsided and I heard them speak.

"Don't think you can get away with this just because your father..."

"You aren't going to pull these kinds of stunts with your mother, boy, not if I'm around to stop it..."

"Fighting, hmmmm?"

"Have you been drinking *beer?*"

I could see that I was covered with blood—all kinds of blood. The gash near my temple throbbed.

Outside I could hear the sirens begin to wail.

"Poor eye contact is a sign of low self-esteem, son... *Son!* See, this is what I mean, look at me when I'm talking to you..."

I looked at my mom and then at my brother, avoiding all the rest. There was no point in standing there. I turned my back on them and started up the stairs.

I heard steps behind me. My sister. What could she want now? Something snapped and I thought, doesn't she realize what a chance she's taking?

"Danny, the girls are sleeping in Mother's room. You be quiet and make sure you don't wake them up. Do you understand me?"

I whirled around. My expression almost sent her reeling down the stairs. "Oh... Kay," I hissed.

She shook her head, measured her rage and cocked an eyebrow in an air of easy superiority.

"You spoiled brat. You've been just coasting along all these years, haven't you? Everyone doting on you, pampering you. Well, that's all over now, Daniel. Things are going to be tougher now, the way they were for me and Skip, back before Mother and Daddy had any money. You're not going to get away with this kind of stuff, honey. You try it and I'll send Ronnie up and he'll beat the living daylights out of you."

I already had my back turned. She didn't follow me.

I stood in my mom's doorway. There on the bed was my five year old niece, Karen, and in the port-a-crib, Lucy, aged two. Both of them as cute as could be, looking untroubled and angelic in their sleep. These, after all, were real children. They didn't abuse their parents or destroy property, and they weren't presumptuous enough to assume that they could experience or understand the kind of grief that adults felt. They were cherubs. Bundles of joy... I shut the door.

I sponged the blood off my coat and hung it on the shower curtain rod. I looked at my bloodied, black-headed, impossibly haggard face in the mirror as I began to undress.

I'll send Ronnie up and he'll beat the living daylights out of you.

I screamed. I punched the bathroom mirror, thinking, *hoping* it would break. It didn't. I stormed into my room, my hands and arms pumped murderously. I emptied the bookshelves, hurled my models against the walls, smashed my aquarium, tore books apart, all the while shouting out my grisly threats.

I'd kill them. Kill them all. My stupid family and their crummy, chicken-shit lives. I'd murder every last one of them. The bastards! The bastards! I'd kill them. Kill them all. Starting...

I stopped and looked at my shut bedroom door. Someone was standing right outside. I thought it was poor, beleaguered Ronnie, sent up here to slap me around a bit.

But Ronnie wouldn't have scraped on my door like that. He wouldn't have made that strange little whistle, or laughed that deep, dreampit laugh.

And the world suddenly spun out of alignment. I thought of the girls asleep in the next room.

"No, no," I muttered, my voice small and weak. "It isn't me, is it. Is it me? Is this the disease? Please go away, don't hurt anyone else, please," wondering if even Larry Lorazo had made it home alive. I begged the thing on the other side of the door to disappear back into its grave, its automobile, my mind... wherever it had come from. Begged it to disappear.

It didn't.

TINY ISLANDS

I

On my sixteenth birthday—having renounced God and wanting no more from life than the chance to withdraw into my own private hell and just maybe carve a piece of the outside world into the image of that hell—I spent fifty cents on a fossil trilobite at the gift shop of the Field Museum in Chicago, and decided to submit my fate to its ancient, pristine influence.

School had been out for a week. On the last day of school, my girlfriend of three months, Debbie Shepard, had dumped me for my friend, Curt Decker. In the course of milking all the melodrama I could out of this little tragedy, I'd managed to bore and depress everyone within earshot—including myself—so my first request to the fossil-charm was to clear the faithless ex-girlfriend from my thoughts once and for all. I should probably have been suspicious the moment I realized just how quickly and thoroughly it granted that request.

It was the summer of 1970, and it was our intention to spend the whole summer playing softball, listening to records, hanging around at Cunningham Beach or else just slumming our days away along the DuPage River. The river ran across three forest preserves, along the edges of backyards, through downtown, and behind Cunningham Beach, where its course was broken up by a number of tiny islands, some of which were overgrown with weeds and trees that in the height of summer created an imposing thicket in which we managed to find some of the privacy and isolation we seemed to hunger for so much. We would spend our afternoons swimming and carousing at the beach—which was an old quarry converted into the world's biggest and greenest swimming pool—and then, when the world seemed particularly dull or oppressive, we would head on out to the river and wade to the tiny islands and feel, for fleeting moments at a time, that we truly had escaped.

In reality, we were a fairly childish bunch of sixteen-year-olds. We weren't particularly tough or violent, and it would be another year before drugs would begin to wash over us like a sweet, corrosive perfume. None of us had a driver's license, few of us had anything remotely resembling jobs and I think, for some of us, all we really wanted was to hide out just a little longer before ... well, whatever. Obviously, something had to happen to us sooner or later, and we had the unshakable conviction that this something would be bad. Lifetimes worth of responsibilities, compromises and tragedies awaited us, and these prospects filled us with what threatened to become an all-encompassing dread. I could see it in Kevin MacDonald's eyes, hear it in the halting monotones of Ralph Coleman's voice and in the sad, misanthropic ravings of Curt Decker.

As for me, well, I couldn't understand how I'd held out as long as I had. Three-and-a-half years before, during the Big Snow of '67, while living in another town, I'd gone out snowballing and skitching with some friends and had been attacked by ... well, how can I tell you this in a way that will sound believable? Let's just say that three of my best friends were murdered that night and I subsequently went home and tried to kill myself. My father had just died a few weeks before, and I believe his death had driven me crazy. Here it was, three-and-a-half years later, and I was still convinced I was crazy.

I would sit out on the tiny islands, sometimes with my friends, sometimes alone, and I would try to will myself sane or will the world into something in which I would appear sane. I would gaze into the intricate impression the trilobite had left upon the coin-sized rock, who knows how many hundreds of millions of years ago, and try to create some kind of resonant connection between the life it had led in that distant Cambrian sea, to the life it was now accompanying me through, as though that connection made me a focused unit upon a predictable, benevolent time line.

Meanwhile, I was taking U. S. History in summer school. Every day at noon I would walk Colleen Carlisle home. It was a ten-minute walk, during which we were learning—almost in spite of ourselves—how to talk to each other in ways that neither of us could talk to anyone else in the world. And although Colleen was Ralph Coleman's girlfriend, and Ralph was my best friend, I began to realize that I was falling in love with her and that somehow, something had to be done about it.

One Saturday, two weeks after the beginning of summer school, we were at Cunningham Beach, sitting around on our towels on the lawn near the water. I kept a pained but watchful eye on Colleen and Ralph, trying to learn something from the way they looked and talked to each other. While Curt and Debbie gave each other those long, sweet looks they always wore when they were about to start making out in public, and Ralph argued with Marty Hiatt—for about the thousandth time in my recollection—about who were the best and, conversely, the most overrated guitarists "in the world," Colleen just sat there. Ralph didn't talk to her, didn't acknowledge her presence, didn't even seem to feel the light stroke of her fingertips up and down the center of his back. Colleen kept her soft blue eyes on him, on the water, or upon all the people passing back and forth in front of us, and I kept my eyes on her. It was easy. No one bothered to look at me at all, not even Colleen, although there were moments when I was sure she knew I was looking at her and was posing her prettiest for my benefit. After about a half hour of this shit, I had to get the hell out of there. They all said goodbye as though they couldn't understand why I had to leave at three in the afternoon and told me how much they hated to see me go and all of that. All except Colleen. She wouldn't even look at me.

I went out to one of the tiny islands and just sat there, watching the pockets of soapsuds bob and thicken along the water's edge, unable to think about anything but Colleen.

Above me cumulus clouds crawled across the sky. I lay back on the dirt and searched the edges and shaded interiors and textures of those clouds, not trying to make them appear like something familiar, just trying to lose myself in the curves and convolutions of forms unlike any I'd ever noticed before. My hand, moving about to provide a better cushion for my head, rubbed against something hard and sharp. I sat up hissing in pain, and saw blood flowing from an abrasion on my knuckle. I looked down and saw a slightly smeared drop of my blood, glimmering with reflected sunlight, resting on the crest of a gray, scimitar-shaped rock, half protruding out of the ground. As I alternately sucked my knuckle and then rubbed it on my cutoffs, I looked down at the smeared droplet and the strangely beautiful shape on which it rested. I rubbed the blood away, spreading a red sash down that curving stone blade, and then picked up a stick and began poking away at the dirt around the rock. I suppose I started out with the intention of freeing it, examining it briefly and then tossing it in the water.

Evidently, some time passed.

"What are you doing?"

I turned around with a gasp.

"Oh, god, Danny, I didn't mean to scare you!"

"You didn't scare me. I was just … what are you doing here?"

"I was up there," pointing up the weed-choked slope that led up to the rear fence of Cunningham Beach, "walking home, and I thought I saw you. It was hard to tell … the leaves and weeds are really thick out here."

"I know. That's what I love about this island. This one in particular."

She knelt at my side. Her blonde, corkscrew curls brushed against my unshirted shoulder for just an instant. She laid her hands over the top of the rock I had been unearthing and petted it gently, far more gently than she had Ralph's back. I looked at that perfect hand, and then, in its wake, at the form across which it had passed.

Had I done this? Could this possibly be the same rock I'd cut my hand on, the same small, single-curved piece I'd been poking around? With its curves, its jointed segments, it didn't resemble a rock at all.

Colleen ran off and then returned immediately with water cupped in her hands. Her arm brushed warm against my own as she sat beside me and released the water onto the stone. The surface beneath the thin layer of dirt was a light, fleshy pink, scattered with red and violet specks ranging in size from sugar granules to pennies. It was made up of two graceful, slightly asymmetrical arcs with a multi-faceted nodule rising at its center. Was it bone? A buried statue? It looked like raw, diseased flesh but it felt cool and polished, like porcelain.

"We can't tell anybody about this," I told her.

"Why not? It's so beautiful."

"Well, then, let's just not tell anybody about it yet. Okay? Let's … dig out the whole thing first, okay?"

"You and me?" she stared right into my eyes, and then nodded her head slowly. "Okay."

But of course it didn't work out that way. Neither of us went back to the island for almost another week. When I finally went out there myself, and sat digging with my fingers and occasionally a short sharp-edged stick, no more than a half hour passed before I heard splashes behind me and turned to see Colleen and Ralph, hand in hand.

"Hey, Pickett, what's goin' on?"

I didn't answer. I just stepped away from my handiwork and watched Colleen's eyes and mouth widen in wonderment, and watched Ralph kneel and squint with a visage of measured disbelief.

"Holy shit, he said. "What the fuck is this?"

I looked back and forth from my friends to the thing rising out of the ground at my feet and made an introduction. "It's the Trilobite Man."

And so my plan for creating a perfect rendezvous for Colleen and me faltered before it ever started. I spent the rest of that afternoon clawing away with my fingers and poking away with a stubby twig, slowly revealing more and more of the figure—it was no longer merely a form—while Colleen watched and sometimes helped and while Ralph sometimes watched and sometimes tried to distract Colleen with some half-hearted attempt at a conversation.

I ignored them both, preferring instead to uncover the Trilobite Man's cold, meat-colored ribs.

For the next couple of weeks I spent every afternoon out there. Almost every day somebody joined me, though no one besides Colleen ever lent a hand in the digging. And, of course, even though he never paid any attention to her unless it was just the three of us, Ralph never let her set foot on the island without him.

I don't know ... At what point did I start to notice the change? Did I accept it all at once or just gradually surrender myself to it, and how long afterward did it take everyone else to notice it? My life up until now had consisted of so many impacted pockets of strange, deathlike dislocations, deluded fantasies of revenge and of my father returning to me after all these years. And of course there was my memory of the man—the thing— that had killed my friends three-and-a-half years before, and the savage beating I'd received, which the world saw as a brutal but botched suicide attempt. Looking at it from that perspective it would have been so easy to dismiss it as just another fantasy, just another example of me withdrawing from the world that had left me so unanchored and raw and Godless. But it was more than that.

Something happened to me and my friends—to the world— once we crossed the narrow stretch of river onto the banks of the tiny island. Sounds that I could not hear beyond that shoreline would swell up from nowhere the moment I stepped on the island, the sounds of millions of hunting, hovering or digging insects, each of whose cries seemed unique from all the rest, but who, as a group, formed a hypnotically resonant harmony in which tones seemed to waiver and bend in unison. If it was raining, the rain always seemed to be of a different character and consistency upon the island—warmer, more aromatic, and, in the sound of its impact upon the leaves and dirt, somehow possessed of a songlike quality of its own. I would stand on the open edge of the island, the rain roaring down on me as though it were a single living entity, reaching down for the sole purpose of calming and reassuring me. The world beyond the edges of the island always seemed a little less colorful, as though all that color was being sucked onto the island itself, enriching the blues and greens of the leaves and grasses, the

gemlike glint of its stones, the protective covering of the island's
single great weeping willow tree and the blood-suffused hues
of the Trilobite Man.

But, of course, none of this was visible from even as close
as fifteen feet—the distance from the river's edge to the island.
It was just another tiny island. And when we ourselves were
off the island, we never talked about it in any way that would
indicate that it held any special power over us.

Even Colleen and I, alone together every weekday at noon
as I walked her home from school, never mentioned the island
or the Trilobite Man. Instead, I would let her look at my poetry,
and we'd both pretend that none of its heartfelt but shameless
clichés were directed at anyone in particular, or I would show
her the panels of the underground comic I was scribbling away
at during those three-hour U. S. History lectures. I would speak
carefully, trying to mold myself with every word and gesture
into everything I knew Ralph wasn't. She got to the point where
she would complain about him and I would comfort her to the
razor's edge of making an outright overture to her.

So, by mid-July I was hopelessly in love with Colleen and
couldn't stop thinking of her except for those moments when I
was on the island, when she became—if only because of Ralph's
presence—just another castaway, just another being lost in
the bewitching folds and breezes that held this island-world
together.

"There." I stood and brushed my dirty hands on my jeans.

I had been digging for several days—in my slow, deliberate
fashion—at a massive form that appeared to be the Trilobite
Man's head.

They all gathered around me, looking down at the crowning
bulk. The Trilobite Man had, up until this point, not exhibited
any hint of symmetry. But now, as we looked down at it, there
seemed to be an overwhelming sense of form. It was still far
from symmetrical and its trilobite-like segments were really
more like a tangle of ribs, all of varying lengths and thicknesses.
Some of them were as thick as human limb-bones and rode over
the top at severe angles to all the rest, and one could easily see
them as appendages—as true arms and legs. The crown was

thick and rounded, except for two long, sharp prongs that extended down from the sides and thinned down and mingled into the latticework of ribs. Upon its bulbous peak were five smooth fissures that extended at least three inches into it.

We looked down at it, especially into those holes, and for the first time could feel it staring back at us.

II

It was a luscious, hanging fly ball, and I could see by its trajectory that it was going to come down about twenty feet behind Marty Hiatt, practically into the street between the park and the train depot.

"Back up, Marty, this one's yours!" I shouted.

Marty sprang to life like someone awakening from a nightmare, skinny arms flailing, his long hair sweeping over his face, as he began running back, still not quite sure where he and the ball should rendezvous.

Well, he tried. He leaped into the air, the ball came crashing down on the hood of Amazing Grace's pickup truck, and Marty landed on top of it, bouncing against metal and then rolling, dazed, down into the grass, while the ball came tumbling after him.

"HEY!" it was Amazing Grace (Jumbo to his friends), all three hundred pounds of him, coming out from the Parkside Tavern. Amazing was one of the town's most notorious rednecks, a hard-drinking, shit-kicking good-ol-boy.

"You little faggot! What the fuck are you doin' ta my truck?"

Amazing Grace was moving fast. Marty got up, grabbed the ball, and backed away in a total panic.

Kevin ran up behind me and poked a finger into my shoulder blade. "Oh shit, oh shit," he whispered.

Amazing stopped and looked at the hood of his blue pickup and then at Marty. "Come here, boy!"

Marty turned tail and ran towards us, but Amazing Grace, who, after all, was far more Amazing than he was Jumbo, managed to charge after Marty and catch him before he reached us.

Out of the corner of my eye I saw a police car pulling up the adjacent street, making his circuit. If only he could just turn the corner now and see ...

Amazing Grace swung Marty around, towering over him, roaring a wave of drunken obscenities down at him and raising that big arm to backhand him.

We were on him as a group, surrounding him and shouting our loudest, darkest threats while Curt jumped into the center of it all, brandishing the baseball bat. Amazing backed off and turned to see the cop car pulling up alongside us. He put up his hand and motioned the cop over to us. The car stopped and a cop got out. As the car door shut I read the motto decaled there: "We care. We enforce."

"Hey, Jumbo, what's the problem?"

"Jim, these boys were jumpin' all over my pickup and when I told them to get off they tried to all take me on at once. And this carrot-headed one here tried to swat me with that bat."

The cop just turned to us, one of those quick, barnyard-chicken-like moves that adults used when they were handed an unexpected revelation of the worst kind about you.

"What's your problem boys? Smoking dope? Getting a little crazy? Do you want me to run you all downtown?"

Amazing Grace just laughed and Jim the cop smiled at him before turning an even more severe face back to us.

"We were just playing ball, officer," Mike Kinney piped in.

"I went after this ball and I just ... fell on his hood," Marty shrugged, realizing the only way to get the rest of us out of this was to make himself look like a total idiot.

"Yeah, and this guy comes spilling out of the bar and screaming at us!" Kevin offered.

Curt threw the bat on the ground. "Of course, if you guys are buddies, by all means! Throw our asses in jail!"

The cop stepped up to Curt and jabbed an outstretched finger before the boy's freckly face. "Hey, son! I'll do just that if I hear any more of that kind of talk!"

"Teach 'em a lesson, Jimmy," Amazing Grace said, sounding

as though he had a mouthful of half-chewed banana.

"Jumbo, why don't you just go on home and let me take care of this, okay?"

Amazing Grace shrugged and said okay. He reached down, picked up the bat—*my* bat, got into the truck and drove away. When he was gone the cop turned back to us.

"If I hadn't stopped when I did you know what would have happened to you? Little guys like you taking on Jumbo Grace? He'd of snatched that bat out of your hands, busted it over his knee and then done the same to the rest of you. And hey! There wouldn't have been a damn thing you could have done about it. I gotta tell you boys, I don't think either of your stories sounded too good, but from what I could see when I drove up, you guys were ganging up on an adult … and you had a baseball bat. Any other town, any other circumstances, and they'd call that a bunch of punks trying to roll a drunk. I'm gonna let you go this time, just because I don't think I've ever seen any of you before, but I want your names, and I want you to know I'm going to remember your faces."

And that was it. I asked why he let the guy off with my baseball bat, and the cop suggested I go see Jumbo myself and ask for it. It wasn't until he got back into the car that I noticed there had been a second cop, sitting in the passenger seat and grinning at the whole thing. They both waved as they drove away.

"What a cocksucker!" cried Jack Kelleher.

"Which cocksucker are you referring to," Kevin asked, "those redneck assholes or the Human Torch here?"

"Hey," Curt hissed, "at least I didn't just stand here waiting for them to slap my hand!"

I turned on Curt and pointed my finger in his face, not much differently than the cop had. "No, man! You just decided to throw a tantrum! He wouldn't have taken my bat if you hadn't thrown it on the fucking ground!"

Ralph looked down at Marty. "You okay, Marty?"

Marty just stood there, looking like a guy who absolutely refused to cry, no matter what. He turned away and waved us off.

"I'm going home. I'll see you tomorrow."

We just stood there quietly for a while, watching Marty retreat and finally disappear around a corner.

"Amazing Grace," Ralph said in disbelief.

"I'd like to kill the motherfucker," Kevin hissed.

Something ugly awoke deep in my gut and rose up into my skull, making my face burn and my teeth grind. I felt as though I'd awakened from a three-and-a-half-year dream.

It was a perfectly normal summer weekday. I walked Colleen home, went home myself, ate, changed and headed off for an afternoon at Cunningham Beach. When I stepped out of the locker room I saw the usual gang of idiots all sitting around a picnic table near the concession stand.

The moment I reached them I realized something was wrong. Their faces just hung there, eyes drooping, mouths defiantly shut. Marty's girlfriend Sue was crying, and Debbie and Colleen huddled on either side of her, stroking her hands and gently shushing her.

"What happened?"

It was Ralph who looked up at me first. "Marty's in the hospital. He got beat up."

"MARTY?"

Kevin stood and looked me in the eye. "Amazing Grace."

And so I heard the story: Marty had been walking home alone from Sue's house at around ten o'clock the night before, when Amazing Grace pulled up in his pickup truck, got out, and, four blocks from Marty's house, beat the shit out of him. Broke his nose, pulled his neck out of joint, and busted two ribs.

And then he drove Marty home, dragged him out of the back of the pickup and up to the front door, and proceeded to tell Mr. and Mrs. Hiatt that their son had been harassing him ever since an altercation at Burlington Park a couple of weeks before, had been shouting insults to him and throwing rocks at his truck. Tonight he'd hit the windshield with a rock and almost sent Amazing's truck into a tree. When Amazing got out of the truck, all shaken up, Marty continued howling and throwing things at him, and so Amazing gave chase. Caught him. And "defended" himself.

"So Marty gets taken to the hospital, the Hiatts go with Amazing Grace down to the cop station, but they don't press charges. Seems the police believed his story. And the Hiatts, the fucking Hiatts, they end up believing it, too." Kevin, who'd been Marty's best friend since kindergarten, shook his head. "You should hear them. They told me they thought Marty would learn a valuable lesson from all this."

Kevin punched the picnic table.

"Can you believe this?" Curt said. "How can they live with him and be stupid enough to believe a story like that?"

And so we just poured out all our bitterness against our parents. All of us had problems, real or imagined, with our parents, and it was the only subject about which we always seemed able to speak with any kind of passionate indignation. Every injustice we saw in another's parents became our own. The Hiatts had committed the most perverse one of all: not knowing their son, not believing in him, not sticking up for him. It didn't matter whether they believed that Marty, peaceful, polite and studious, could have harassed a three-hundred pound shit-kicker so mercilessly, or whether they were just as afraid of Amazing Grace as we were. A real father or mother would have stood up for Marty. Wouldn't they?

We decided to go visit him at the hospital. It was a long, desperate trudge, and every vehicle that passed us inspired a seething rage in us.

Of course, it was the violation that made us smell blood, that made us so hungry for revenge. Had it been a kid at school it would have been different. But Amazing Grace was at least thirty years old. An adult. We seethed because, in reality, this all just confirmed our most melodramatic visions of ourselves and the adult world we despised so much. It wasn't a game. Adults really were tainted and cruel and all in it together.

That night I ate at Curt's house. Afterwards we picked up Mike Kinney and Jack Kelleher at Cunningham Beach and all four of us went down to the river.

And onto the island.

There were mosquitoes all around the river but there were

no mosquitoes on the island. The air smelled of sewage down by the river but the odors on the island were sweet and alive and seemed to be somehow connected to the melodies that whispered up from the depths the lush, snaking vegetation that grew along its soft, crystal-dotted shore. Near the north edge of the island, just outside the reach of the Great Weeper, lay the Trilobite Man.

For a while we had treated it as a joke, putting glasses onto that great but bulbous globe we believed to be its head, trying to create symmetry and physique in that matrix of sinews and segments and bold, dimpled ganglia by laying out pants and shirts and shoes around it. It was never very funny. We would strip that stuff away and then see it for what it really was. What it was really becoming.

The sun was turning a rich, eye-imprinting orange. The translucent pink and red surface of the Trilobite Man seemed to absorb that orange and hold it deep inside, where it escaped only as graceful, pulsing glimmers.

Kevin and Ralph showed up about half an hour after we did, brandishing a bottle of bourbon. Mike, Jack and Curt took off after a couple of convulsive, obligatory swallows.

It was soon apparent that Kevin wanted to kill off the bourbon in a hurry, and so we followed him about the island, taking an occasional swig. He raved about the injustice of the world and how tough it was to be a really obnoxious guy whom girls just didn't understand. All the while the landscape around us, not even big enough to be a decent-sized backyard, seemed to open up to accommodate our wanderings, so that we stepped out from under the protection of the Great Weeper to look out on what, in our ever-drunkening state, seemed like a limitless peninsula along a still and shimmering sea. At its center was the desiccated corpse of the Trilobite Man, upon whose shell and bones and tendons the moonlight played dazzling, impossible tricks. The air around us filled with the buzzing songs of great, ancient insects, and those songs comforted us, gave us a sense of protection while the whiskey gave us a sense of strength.

Kevin killed off the bottle and almost immediately began puking his guts out. Ralph and I spent the next hour walking

Kevin around, trying to figure out how to get him into good enough shape to walk home. In the end we had to give it up. He slumped in the long grass, moaning, his skin cold and wet, and quaking with nausea. Ralph and I just sat there, listening to him mumble, occasionally laughing if something sounded funny, but mainly just staying quiet. We didn't talk about Marty. We didn't talk about Colleen. Ralph had been my best friend since I'd moved here, and now I couldn't even bring myself to talk to him. And since he couldn't either, I guessed that he knew everything, which made it even more impossible to talk. Eventually we decided that Kevin wouldn't be able to go home tonight. I offered to look after him, so Ralph just gave a relieved shrug and left me there.

So I just sat there on the island. In between Kevin and me was the Trilobite Man, whom I watched gleaming in the moonlight, an impossible configuration of forms, beyond life and death and art, like a great geological secret rising up from the depths of the earth offering some kind of elusive salvation for us alone. What was the Trilobite Man? Why didn't we ever ask that question anymore? Was it because we were embarrassed not to know, or afraid because we did know and did not dare to mention it?

On the other side of the Trilobite Man, Kevin's drunken moaning seemed to take on an almost religious tone, as though the complex forms glowing in the moonlight were a gigantic, labyrinthine temple, and the moans were the choruses of the throngs of believers moving in its shadows.

The ground underneath me rolled and breathed and quivered. The epicenter was the Trilobite Man and those swelling, dirge-like choruses were coming from Kevin, but it appeared that the whole thing, the unstable dance of the ground beneath me and the low, mournful chants, was directed solely at me, as though I had to clear something useless away from my eyes and ears in order to know what was truly happening around me.

I placed my hand on the Trilobite Man, running my palm across its knotted limbs and threads and over its swelling ganglia. It was warm and wet and sometimes it even appeared to throb and shudder.

After a while the sounds and rumbling grew so violent I wanted to get the hell off the island. But when I looked around me, I saw nothing beyond the shore, no river, no rocks, just an obstructing blackness that held me snug within it.

Kevin awoke soon after sunrise. He stood with a start and asked me what happened.

"I couldn't get you off the fucking island, man. So I just let you stay here."

"And you watched over me all night? My hero! "

"Can you make it out of here all right now?"

"Yeah, I ... I ..." He winced and rubbed his forehead, and then his face. He looked down at the Trilobite Man. It was cold and polished and lifeless.

"Oh, shit, did I have some weird dreams."

"Really? Like what?"

He stepped around the "body," looking at it as though for the first time.

"I don't know. Just some weird fucking dreams is all. Did you get any sleep?"

"Naah, I couldn't sleep."

And then we just hopped across the little rock bridge and back into the old world. I felt a strange, unaccountable loss the moment we hit shore.

III

On the day Marty was finally well enough to go back to Cunningham Beach, I invited him over for dinner. When we got to my house my sister Jeannine was on the porch waiting for us. As soon as she saw us she began screaming.

Inside the house my mom was crying hysterically and shouting curses at Jeannine. Marty stepped in our door, thinking he might use the phone to call his folks, but thought better of it when he heard my mom and sister both filling the house with howls of angry hysteria.

I'll be honest. My mom and sister had had a pretty fucked-up time of it the past few years, what with my dad dying and leaving us with no money and Ronnie splitting and leaving Jeannine with no money and the two of them and me and Jeannine's little daughters all crammed into this house together against our will. There was never enough money, they were lonely, they'd never gotten along, and the world just seemed to be dropping misfortune after misfortune into their paths in the forms of humiliating jobs, old cars that never ran, insulting relatives and neighbors. But my problem with them always seemed to stem from the fact that in their dealings with me, I seemed to be the focus, the quintessential insult in their tragic lives. I was ugly, I was lazy, I was hairy, I was male, I was lazy, I was a horrifyingly bad influence on her two little girls, and most of all, I was just damned lazy. The only way they seemed able to end a fight with each other was to start in on me.

"I hope you're proud of yourself, you lazy rat!" one of them (it didn't matter whom) screamed at me as I stood there in the doorway, pondering the wisdom of asking what was for dinner.

My mom just kept looking at me, shaking her tear-blotched head, and Jeannine kept pacing the house, slamming things, stopping every once in a while in front of me to deliver a new and improved threat and insult into my face.

"I should have seen this coming the moment I let you and mother move in with us! I should have known it! How daaarreee you bring this kind of dirt and ruin into my house, how dare you show your face here!" As usual, I had no idea what she was talking about. "You're sick, Danny, and all of your friends are sick, and I wouldn't be surprised if you started killing them off the way you killed all your friends in Hillside!!"

"Jeannine!" my mom cried, rushing forward to stop her and then thinking better of it and running off into the kitchen. "What's that supposed to mean?"

She got this crazy, I'm-going-out-on-a-limb-and-it-feels-great kind of smile on her face and stepped forward, realizing she'd hit a raw nerve. Or maybe she was just letting loose a suspicion she'd had all along.

"You and me don't have to kid each other, do we, Danny?" Her voice was soft and almost seductive now. "I know about you."

"What do you know about me?"

"I know what you ARE!" screaming the last word into my face.

I grabbed her by the shoulders and shook her. "What do you know about me? Huh? Huh? WHAT AM I?"

I could hear Karen and Lucy crying in the background. Jeannine's eyes glazed wide and she let out a bloodcurdling scream, a scream she meant to be heard all over the neighborhood.

I let go and started to run out the door. I saw the two girls and I stopped and kneeled to them. Lucy ran away, but Karen, who had just turned nine and was the closest thing I had to a friend in that house just stood there, looking at me with a sad, tear-smeared face.

"Karen, what do you think I am?"

"KAREN, YOU STAY AWAY FROM HIM!!"

"Huh, Karen? Tell me, will you?"

"Oh, Danny," she sobbed, shaking her head so sweetly at

me. "Please go away."

I ran from the house. I ran all the way down Ellsworth Avenue until I reached the college field, where I collapsed on a hilltop and rolled around in the freshly cut grass, looking up into the violently carved clouds drifting over me. I had to go somewhere. The island? No, no, not after what my sister had said. I should have just gone home with Marty.

When I finally got up I headed past the Field House and the playing fields, towards Colleen Carlisle's house.

Colleen answered the door. She looked around to see where her parents were and then stepped out onto the porch. "Danny … what's up?"

I shrugged.

"Do you want to come in?"

"Not really. Can you come out? I've got to talk to you." I hadn't seen her since summer school had let out. She and Ralph had been having all kinds of problems, and instead of that bringing the two of us closer together, it had pushed her away from the core of the group and almost out of my reach altogether.

She hesitated. Oh, god, she knew. Of course she knew. "Okay. Can we go over to Curt's? Debbie and Sue are over there."

"Sure, sure, whatever."

She told her folks she was leaving and then we set off. I wanted so much just to spill it all then, about how she was all I could think about, how I'd do anything for her, how I couldn't live without her and would never in all my life stop loving her. But Colleen kept the conversation going all by herself, talking about how she'd had just about enough of that bastard Ralph and about a series of paintings she was going to start and had I ever thought about doing something besides cartooning because she really thought I'd like oil painting and how badly she wanted to go away and study ballet while her father wanted her to go into the hard sciences, like her older sister.

So I just listened dutifully, interested in everything she said because the words emerging from her lips were just for me, as they'd been on all those walks home from summer school.

We passed by Burger King, where a bunch of kids, most of

them older than us, were hanging around the bridge, looking scary. Someone behind us shouted, "Nice tits, sweetheart!"

His friends all laughed. I whirled around, not even sure who'd said it. "Hey, FUCK YOU!"

Colleen grabbed my arm. "Danny, come on."

Todd Delaney stepped away from the crowd. He was a couple of inches taller than me—about six foot—and was almost as skinny as I was, but he was nineteen and he'd been in jail already and he had a reputation as a wild and cruel street fighter.

"What did you say to me, little boy?"

I didn't answer.

He stepped up to me, displaying a mouthful of snaggled and discolored teeth. He reached up casually and grabbed hold of my nose, pinching it and refusing to let go. His friends all laughed.

Maybe he wasn't expecting me to punch him, or tackle him afterwards, because in the next few seconds I made Todd Delaney look real bad, sending his head cracking onto the concrete in front of the bridge. My fists were flailing and there seemed to be no doubt in my mind that I was going to put this low-life away. I don't know when or how it all turned bad on me, but after the dust cleared I was dazed and bleeding and Todd had me on my feet, leaning me backwards over the bridge's edge with his palm on my face, telling me that if he ever saw me near the bridge again he was going to throw me over the edge.

And then he just hurled me away. I collapsed in the Burger King parking lot and rolled up to Colleen's feet. There were about a dozen of them back there, laughing. I looked at Colleen, stood and walked away, for the moment not caring if she followed or not, not caring whether I ever uttered another word or looked into another face for the rest of my miserable life.

But Colleen had her arm around me, she was palming my cheek and turning my face so she could look at me. She was not disgusted by my outburst or disillusioned at the poor showing I made in defense of her honor. When we got a couple of blocks away from the scene of my humiliation I stopped and turned to her, standing close and dropping my head toward her, almost close enough to kiss her.

"I can't go to Curt's. I just ... not after ..."

She took my hand. "All right, where do you want to go?"

"I want to go to the island."

There were all kinds of conflicting forces at work behind her face now, straining and illuminating her features.

"Okay."

She let go of my hand, and did not say another word to me all the way there.

When I stepped onto the island I felt the air change, heard the strange but now familiar calls of the birds and insects that seemed to live there and nowhere else in the world.

I reached in my pocket and pulled out my fossil trilobite. Thank you for finally pulling it all together, thank you for making it all clear, at last ...

IV

The sounds that rose from the rocks and grasses and from the interlacing, gently rocking tree limbs and from within the canopy of the Great Weeper were all living sounds—speaking, singing sounds, a complex, repeating pattern carried on the breezes and then rising upwards into a sky so full of stars and lacy nebulae that it truly did resemble a lush fabric ceiling, the gentle, protective, dark-gloved palm of God sheltering us from the brutal but pathetically brittle world we had just left.

I tried sitting in the grass, but the moment I kneeled, my ribs exploded with pain, so I stumbled and collapsed instead. Colleen was next to me in a second, helping me sit up. Her hand rested on my right forearm as she sat directly across from me, still looking up at the sky but pausing for longer and longer stares into my own eyes.

"It's so beautiful. I've never seen a sky like this ... Not even out in the country ... it's almost ..."

"No, not almost. It is." Oh, shit, I thought, here it comes! "I wish we never had to leave this island. I wish we could just stay here forever, never have to face any of them ever again, never have to ..."

I shook my head. It seemed that the number of things I needed to escape from was too enormous to express. Her hand tightened around my wrist. I looked over her shoulder and saw the Trilobite Man lying in the dirt, staring up into the stars with his black, gaping eyes.

She let out a nervous laugh. "Sometimes I don't understand what I'm doing, like everything in the whole world is just a big mistake and I'm not a part of it, not even supposed to be a part of it. But every time I think about running away I start thinking ... where would I be running away to? I mean, where do I go if I don't want to do any of it?"

"You can stay here." Out beyond the Trilobite Man, beyond the Great Weeper, the landscape seemed to spread out forever, an unblemished patterning of island and ocean stretching out towards a haze-blanketed horizon. "With me."

She took her hand away. The ground beneath me seemed to be moving, groaning lightly, as though awakening from a long sleep.

"I wish I could." She looked down at the water lapping against the rocks. "You're the only one in the world who understands me anymore. Sometimes I ... feel so bad about you."

"Huh?"

"Because of Debbie and Curt, because of Ralph, because of me. Danny, I know about you ... the way you ... I've been afraid all this time, because I'm just so crazy about Ralph and he doesn't ... want anything to do with me anymore. And you're always there. Your voice is always so soft for me, and never for anyone else. It's like you're a completely different person for me. I don't ... deserve this."

I touched her cheek with the fingertips of my right hand. It was still a soft, babyish cheek. Her face glowed beneath all those lights while the moonlight broke up on the lapping water and reflected in her eyes as sharp, electrical glimmers. It seemed to me now that all I'd ever really wanted in this lonely fiasco of a life was this moment, to be alone with this girl and to prove to her all that she seemed unable to see.

"Colleen, I adore you. I'm absolutely crazy about you." My palm went flat against her cheek and my fingers found the back of her neck, which Ralph had once inadvertently informed me was the most ticklish part of her body. She shut her eyes and I could feel her holding back the tremble.

Beneath me the ground rolled and shook in a series of shock waves, spreading out from the enthroned grave of my only God.

I had the trilobite fossil in my other hand. I placed it in her upturned palm.

"What's this?"

"It's yours. I want you to have it."

She looked down at it, refusing to show me her face.

"It's the fossil. Your trilobite. You can't give me this. This is ..."

She looked up at me suddenly, as though trying to scoop something out of me with those eyes.

"I'll be anything you want me to be. I know I'm a fuck-up and I know the way those guys all talk about me, but that doesn't matter anymore. Everything is different because of you. I'm different. I swear I am. Just give me the chance to prove it to you."

"Do you love me?"

"Yes."

"Then tell me. I want to hear you tell me that."

"I love you, Colleen Carlisle. Okay? Do you want to hear it again?" I was probably getting a bit drunk on all this. "I'll shout it so the whole world can hear it."

And then she kissed me. Her lips and tongue were soft and moist at first, and then they seemed not to exist as separate entities at all. It was just the two of us, our faces connected by the desperate fusing of soft tissues between and within us. I would have to say, all pecks and slobbers and hickeys and drooling chewers aside, it was the first real kiss of my entire life. I could feel her exhale into my face, could hear her sigh and knew at once what that sigh meant as she scooted closer and put her arms around me.

And then we heard it. We pulled apart and looked around us at the glimmering island. The ground movement, which had seemed like mere extensions of that momentum between us, had stopped suddenly. Behind Colleen there was a swirling of light rising from the ground. I pulled her towards me and turned her around.

We both saw it stand. Neither of us screamed or tried to crawl away. We both froze, no longer two individuals with lives and priorities and problems or even identities. It seemed to suck all that away from us as it rose before the gigantic moon, so beautiful, so graceful, so much more than a collection of ribs and tendons and incomprehensible tangles.

Had I stood and tried to touch him, I'm not even sure if my hands would have rested upon any surface or whether they would have just drifted on through intertwining strands of liquid light. He seemed possessed of no definitive, contiguous form, but rather seemed like a series of similar but distinctive images cross-dissolving, one into the other, sometimes sharp and focused, and sometimes obscured by swirls of haze and white, snaking smoke. At one moment he almost appeared to be a man, but that illusion was lost in the next moment, when he seemed to resemble a glass Scorpion fish, a dimly perceived figure within a mass of sharp, threatening barbs. Forms seemed to grow and wrestle their way out of his core, each one overpowering the last only to be pushed away or swallowed or dissipated by the next. But this was surely the Trilobite Man, the thing I had spent the summer lovingly unearthing with my bare hands, around which we'd spent so many days and evenings, withdrawing deeper and deeper into the world that was now so clearly weaved by the Trilobite Man himself. It was a world in his own image: a reflector of broken, dancing light, ever changing, more hypnotic and all-encompassing as it drew power from … where? From the moon? From us?

Or was it only me?

The moment I admitted this possibility to myself, the Trilobite Man seemed to twist in space and suspend within its anatomic maelstrom the semblance of a face, a face that for just an instant struck a familiar, horrible chord within me. But there were thousands of faces there, and then none at all, as it twisted again and arched its body beneath the moon while two great appendages rose from its mass and grasped for the moon, or maybe for something greater and farther and more impossible to reach than our simple, tarnished moon.

And then I heard the shouts. I tried to tell myself that they were merely another variation on the animal sounds that filled the night around me. But they were familiar sounds, and they were getting louder by the moment. Colleen and I sat up.

They were running along the pathway, then stumbling down the slope towards the river's edge, breathing in desperate gasps. I saw dark shapes splashing across the shallow river. I pushed Colleen back under the drooping branches of the Great Weeper and then watched as Kevin and Ralph leaped up onto the island, their faces full of terror.

"What the hell are you guys so—"

And then I heard another shout.

"You can't hide from me you dirty little motherfuckers!!"

Amazing Grace. It couldn't be! I looked around. No glimmering canopy, no ocean stretching to the horizon. No Trilobite Man. And no moon.

He charged across the river, shouting like a man chasing the last barrier between himself and starvation, hungry, savage and completely crazy. He fell into the river, roared as he pushed himself up and then staggered, breathless, dripping and wild-eyed onto the island.

In his hand was a baseball bat. My baseball bat.

"You sons-a-bitches think you're pretty damned funny, doncha? Huh? Doncha? Funny and smart and too fast and just too fucking clever for me, huh?" The air filled with the stench of beer belches and body odor. I looked around me and saw, for what seemed like the first time I my life, the flood lights illuminating Cunningham Beach, the headlights over on Aurora Avenue that backlit the power lines that ran along that road.

We did not run. We just spread out, trying to keep a little distance from each other and the bat. This is how people die. How could I have forgotten this?

"That's my bat, sir," I blurted, feeling a little nauseous and giddy, "That's my bat and I want it back."

"You want it back, huh? Catch!"

He lunged forward. There was no mistaking his intent. I jumped out of his way and fell backwards over something that was just now rising from the ground.

The Trilobite Man was still the same flurry of glimmering lights and ghostly, transparent barbs in which solid flesh and bone seemed to dance a ferocious metamorphic dance. As an overall form he was vague and confusing, but there was no confusing what he did to Amazing Grace.

He skewered the fat man where he stood, driving a thick,

pointed glass appendage into the man's crotch and up through his body until it emerged out of the broad (and broadening) forehead, where the tip seemed to soften, twisting around wormlike for a moment and then receding back into the head. By this time Amazing Grace's feet were off the ground, kicking in a desperate attempt to reach the dirt again. The night filled with his screams, the screams of a man very much alive.

He was screaming for us to help him.

I looked around. No more flood lights, streetlights, headlights, power lines, only a swollen moon low in the sky and a chorus of laughing insects applauding Amazing Grace's performance.

The bat flew out of his hand and caught Ralph in the temple. Ralph went down. Colleen darted out from the Great Weeper and kneeled at his side.

Something that I swear to you was *not* me convulsed inside of me at that moment and I reached down for the bat, the Louisville Slugger my dad had bought for my twelfth birthday.

The mighty arm or leg or tail or whatever it was, twisted this way and that, playing with the thrashing, screaming man skewered upon it. Amazing Grace looked into my face and I could see, in the bloody mess spreading out over it, the desperate pleading of a small child.

I wiped the desperation off his face with the baseball bat. I hit him hard enough to send any man flat on his back, but Amazing Grace had all kinds of support now and it was no problem for me to haul off and swing the bat a second time, as though his head were the juiciest slow-pitch in the history of softball. I did not miss. Once I followed through and turned back to him, there was very little left of Amazing Grace's head.

Somebody screamed. I guess it was probably Colleen.

I began beating Amazing Grace's huge body until the bat splintered in half. Somewhere along the line Kevin got a hold of the smaller half and we were both pounding away at the thing that only a moment ago had been a ferocious, drunken man whose only intent was to kill us. Now he was something less than a body. I remember the moment at which he plopped into the dirt but I don't think I understood what that meant at the time. I stabbed some part of him (it didn't really matter which part by this time) and began jumping up and down on him. I was screaming curses but I don't know if they were directed towards Amazing Grace or even if they were made up of words. I know only that I was not alone in this. Kevin was there, too, screaming and tearing away at the flesh, trying to obliterate all traces of that thing that, hard to believe, had once been a man.

It was exhaustion that stopped us. I don't know who went down first. All I know is that I was sitting up and looking at what seemed almost like a mirror image of myself. It was Kevin, sitting up and looking back at me. In between us, spread out through the rocks and dirt, was a bubbling, hissing mass of bone and flesh and viscera and—so it seemed—something more, something still alive, swimming noisily within it all.

I turned around and saw Colleen and Ralph. Her head was bowed and she was crying. She refused to look at us. Ralph, covered with blood that surely was not his own, just stared at us, not in horror or disbelief or even anger.

Nothing happened. I stood and all around me were those lights and automobile sounds and the smell of sewage. It had all drained away: the rage, the magic, as well as the Trilobite Man who had threaded it all together.

I looked at Kevin. "Why did you bring him here?"

"I didn't think he'd follow us. I didn't think he could find us here."

I shook my head and motioned around me. "Find us *where?*"

And then I walked away, splashed through the shallows and up the slope and down the path and through town and onto Ellsworth and up to my porch and through the front door and up into the bathroom, where I washed it all away. When I went back downstairs, I found that my sister Jeannine was the only one up. She asked me if I wanted to split a frozen pizza with her. I said sure. We sat there together and she kept me up until four in the morning, explaining life to me.

All four of us showed up at the beach the next day. Ralph and Colleen were back together, in a renewed and somewhat defiant display of affection. Everybody seemed to be in good spirits and we spent an hour and a half over by the high-dive, showing off and generally making idiots out of ourselves.

Not a single word was mentioned about Amazing Grace or the Trilobite Man or the island. All that afternoon, and on almost every afternoon from then until school started, I was sure one of them would quietly bring up the subject to me, but no one did. I could sit across from any of them and talk for hours and I couldn't see it shadow their faces for even a single instant. It was as though it had never happened.

The local paper wasted a lot of ink speculating about the disappearance of Amazing Grace. A police investigation was conducted somewhere along the line, but it never came close to us, not even to Marty Hiatt, who—had he ever considered it—would probably have had as much reason to kill Amazing Grace as anyone in the world.

Junior year was pretty good, got better as it went on, and I even managed to get over Colleen. I grew another two inches and my hair grew another six inches and I guess you could say I turned into a real asshole. A slightly smarter version of Todd Delaney, I'm afraid.

Late the next summer, I went out to the island again, all by myself. Near the shade of the weeping willow there was a shallow form protruding from the ground. It might have been a skeleton, but whether it would have been a man's or not I couldn't say. It might have been Amazing Grace. It could have just as easily been the Trilobite Man. Maybe it was my imagination, or just a complicated tangle of tree roots riding along the ground level.

But there, alongside it, in stark contrast to the dry, clay-lightened dirt, was a small black form, no bigger than a quarter. I picked it up. My fossil trilobite. The creature's delicately etched impression had worn almost completely away. I rubbed it with my thumb and then dropped it into the enigmatic tangle at my feet.

When I stepped to the island's edge I looked up the slope and saw the barbwired top of the chain-link fence that enclosed Cunningham Beach, saw the power lines stretched above it, and heard the shouting of kids at the beach and the droning of hundreds of cars beyond it.

I turned back, retrieved the little black stone, and put it in my pocket.

HORIZON LINE

There was a moment—a single, irretrievable moment—when the numbness that passed for strength and the immobility that passed for resolve vanished, and he wanted to cry out to the young couple in the boat, beg them to take him back. They would have laughed, cursed him, but maybe they would have taken him back to the ship, where he would have been ridiculed and perhaps even arrested for breaching his contract, but ... would have at least been taken away from this horrible place.

I will surely die here, he thought. But what had he expected? He'd envisioned the atoll as something delicate and beautiful, the plants and animals living on it and in the waters within and beyond its borders so exotic, so ... precious. But the rock beneath him was hard and dangerously slick, and the living things so numerous and congested upon and between those rocks that he could not take a single step without crushing something. Fat, shapeless white worms splattered beneath his shoes.

His gear and provisions had all been stowed away in the "cottage"—really the tumbled ruins of what might once have been a lighthouse, overgrown by algae and the plants that rooted among the algae and whatever tiny creatures could nest and hunt within that clinging matrix. The smartest thing would be to go inside, try to straighten it up a little, unpack, lie on the bed and rest until this wave of panic and regret passed. But he was restless, and terrified of the prospect of living so alone on this ring for the next forty days.

So he decided to walk a lap around the atoll. He estimated the diameter to be a little less than a half a mile at its widest point, but he couldn't remember the formula for estimating its circumference. It didn't matter. The band of rock never seemed to widen to more than thirty or forty yards, and it was this distance that mattered most. He was pinned between two bodies of water and there was no place he could go, not even the cottage, to escape their pressure.

The atoll had no name. The Great Southern Ocean was full of such formations, and none of them had names—at least none that were publicly known—and most of the formations themselves were so small that they showed up on no maps that he had ever seen. Their very existence was not widely known; they were merely part of a phenomenon that revealed itself to those in need of it, through untraceable whispers and infiltrated dreams.

Crabs climbed the mosses from out of the ocean, but none ever ventured farther than a few feet from the edge of the rocks. The animals from the lagoon, more primeval and wholly unfamiliar to him, seemed more courageous. With their intricately segmented shells and their cumbersome arrays of legs and feelers, these arthropods—no two of them alike—were like holdovers from some shallow Paleozoic sea.

His footing was awkward and he kept falling, so that by halfway around the atoll he was exhausted and riddled with bruises, abrasions and spasms. But he didn't regret the walk. He needed pain. He needed exhaustion and exasperation.

He looked across the lagoon at the cottage, so small and overgrown that it was barely distinguishable from the plant-choked rocks surrounding it.

He'd made nearly one complete circuit when he saw the mist beginning to rise from the lagoon. It drifted over the water and out towards the ring. The air was warm that day but the mist, once it finally reached the shore and brushed against his cheek, was even warmer. Much warmer. And within those stretches of mist, tendrils of color that appeared almost solid—deep blues and crimsons, pulsed in and out of existence.

By the time he reached the cottage, the mist seemed to have merged into a single, nearly comprehensible form, an organism, an intelligence, diffuse only to maintain its omniscience.

He reached out, grabbed at a patch of mist and closed his

fists on nothing at all. He then forced himself to go inside, unpack and organize his provisions for his ... hermitage, for this self-inflicted punishment for which he had paid every cent he had, every possession he owned, and all traces of an identity that had ceased to exist the moment the boat pulled out of port at journey's beginning.

They were out on the rocks the following morning. Tall, slender, humanoid, and, except for the meager strands of blue and crimson suspended within them, virtually transparent. Dozens of them, rising from the lagoon, diving back into the lagoon, languishing at the edge of the stagnant ocean, their only purpose seemingly to catch and lovingly bend the sunlight as it passed through their bodies, leaving glistening arcs across their surfaces. They were like angels of molten glass, graceful as they stepped and slithered among the plants that lined the rocks, all beneath a sky of pure, unblemished blue. Even without eyes it was obvious that they were all turning to look at him as he stepped out of the cottage, the smaller ones scurrying away, the larger ones slowly shuffling out of his path as he stepped among them. He was enthralled and fearless.

"What do I do now?!" he cried, at them, at the flawless sky and whatever intelligence might reside there—or beneath the surface of the ocean or the lagoon. Forty days—thirty-nine now—to consider his sins, to pinpoint and purge all that was despicable in his nature, which would leave him with ... what? He didn't know how to spend his time and he had no idea what he would end up with when it was all over.

So he walked. Another full circuit around the atoll, every once in a while breaking into a run and only stopping when the footing became too treacherous. By the time he made it back to the cottage he was scraped and bloody and drenched with sweat—the obvious action at this point would have been to strip and bathe in the lagoon, but it was too alive, too active. And the ocean was so dormant—motionless, that in the distance it looked almost like a viscous desert on some dead world.

He went inside the cottage, figuring to eat a little dried fruit and then sleep away the hottest part of the day, but just inside the doorway he discovered one of the Transparents, kneeling before his open traveling bag.

"What the HELL are you doing?" he cried.

He lunged at it, reached for its throat, only in that last instant wondering just what kind of surface he was about to touch—or plunge through.

It seemed almost to evaporate in the instant his hands would have closed around its throat, bathing his fists in an oily mist. It was behind him now, smelling faintly of fish and lagoon water. He whirled, thrashing blindly and catching the Transparent— which was solid after all—across the flank with his elbow. It faltered slightly and he, taking full advantage of that, kicked it out the open door of the cottage.

There. He could have slammed the door, turned away, but instead he looked out and watched the Transparent struggling to pull itself off the rocks. Part of its arm and hip were seeping into the tangle of plants.

He leaped out of the doorway, his feet landing squarely on the chest of the fallen Transparent, half-expecting it to rupture beneath him. It didn't—not yet. He jumped up and down on it, screaming hysterically at the others, stirred on by their cringing retreat. He'd expected them to charge him, tear him apart. He had clearly misunderstood. Beneath his feet the Transparent leaked away, leaving not even color, not even a thin surface membrane. It left behind nothing at all—except a mess on his shoes and pant legs. Its consistency was only slightly thicker than water.

He marched into the cottage and up the stairs, throwing himself on the bed and only then kicking his shoes off and nudging them to the floor. Outside he heard a soft but shrill chorus of whistles. He rolled off the bed and went to the window. Down below, in the spot where he had stomped the Transparent to death, an array of glimmering, oily globules rose from the tangles and rolled—amoeba-like—into the outstretched arms of the Transparents kneeling before it. Seven had come forward to collect the remains in their arms. When they walked away towards the lagoon, the crowd parted for them. As the last of the seven passed, the others fell in behind, until the entire group was entering the lagoon as a single, orchestrated unit. There their forms seemed to merge, to become the water itself, a solitary mass that then disappeared entirely amid the turbulence of an exploding gas bubble.

His first few days were troubled. Still unsure of the ultimate repercussions of killing the Transparent, he didn't leave the second floor of the cottage for three days. He paced, stared out the window, nibbled, and rummaged through the paraphernalia left behind by other pilgrims. Most of the books and journals were decayed beyond recognition. There was an old computer in the corner, draped beneath canvas and encrusted with mold. He shook it from side to side and heard a sickening, sloshing sound from within its shell.

And there was an embroidered notebook, neatly wrapped in plastic and almost perfectly preserved, though its design and the delicate calligraphy that filled its pages seemed to indicate an unimaginable vintage. It was a woman's notebook, a chronicle of the miserable life that had driven her here, and the oppressive sense of scale the ocean, with its all-consuming, 360-degree horizon line, had laid upon her. But she had known the Transparents as well. To her, they were angels of salvation— gentle, watery souls there to douse the smolderings life had scarred her with, to lift and caress her and free her of the gravity that had been tugging her graveward for her entire life.

The moon seemed impossibly large and bright out there. With no reference points on the horizon, should it have appeared so large? Shouldn't it rather have appeared smaller? And the terrain of the moon itself—it was as though it was so close that he could make out each individual hill and valley, along with forests, rivers and great, decaying monsters.

It was the cool night air that finally drew him downstairs and out of the cottage door where he discovered, resting on a particularly elegant formation of rock, a single Transparent, staring at the ocean.

He expected it to slide off the rock and slither back into the water. But it only looked at him with a delicate turn of the head, otherwise remaining motionless. It was small, a child—sexless, unthreatening. Perhaps it was some kind of angel.

When the Transparent turned away, tilting its head towards the moon whose light illuminated its liquid skull, he felt a profound sense of release. He thought of the woman's passionate journal entries. He sat on the rocks, nestling within the wet vegetation and scurrying worms and crustaceans, and he, too, looked up at the moon. And his skull, too, felt as though it were illuminating the night air.

He fell asleep and awoke a few hours later, to the sound of animals killing and devouring each other on the rocks—birds and crabs and other, darker things that had emerged from the lagoon. He was alone.

But when he ventured out after sunset the next night, he found the small Transparent, seated alone on that same rock and staring at the ocean.

As he sat, the Transparent turned and seemed to focus on him intensely. Its colorful organs, glowing with moonlight, pulsed and quivered, sending ripples through its deep, clear flesh.

"I shouldn't be here," he said, not to it or even to himself. "I thought I needed this. I thought I'd … lost all hope and that it was either this or kill myself. I thought: I can give it all up, I can sacrifice my identity and the assurance of ever having a roof over my head once I got back … if it means I don't have to feel that bad ever again. But I was wrong. I don't want to be dead and I don't want to give up everything I've just signed away. I want it back. I'll go see a million therapists, I'll go until I find the one who gives me the right justification, the right excuse, the right prescription to just *pull me out of it*. I don't want to be in this place. It was better being me at my absolute worst than being on this smelly, slimy ring of rock with these … I don't know … HEY! What are you anyway?" shouting at the Transparent. "Some kind of jellyfish, right?"

The Transparent was still looking at him, and for a moment he thought it was going to speak. Within its torso, strands of its organs had encircled into a loose, pulsing knot—a heart.

It rose, stepped up to him and reached out its glimmering arm, palm up. "What?" he asked. But it did not move, did not answer. Reluctantly, he touched the Transparent's hand with his own, felt the other's close on his, and was brought to his feet.

"Where are we going?" knowing exactly where they were going. It led him to the edge of the lagoon and beyond, up to its knees in water while he still perched on the rock.

It yanked at him and he relented for just an instant, and so hit the water belly first, mouth open in the middle of a shout. He sank, touched bottom and stood, coughing and gasping as his head reared out of the water. That water was warm, much warmer than the night air. It felt wonderful but even so, it was only with another tug that he let himself be pulled under again. Once there, it was hard to reconcile the fact that he would ever have to resurface again.

The Transparents were all around him down here, vague and vigorous irregularities in the moonlit water itself. They surrounded him, directed him, and yet when he needed to take a breath, they gently prodded him to the surface.

After that he swam freely, more relaxed than he'd ever felt underwater, examining the mouths of grottoes, the soft translucent tubules that branched through the water like a circulatory system. He watched the schools of fish that swam among those tubule forests and the invertebrates cluttering the bottom. Towards the darkness at the center of the lagoon, movements of light and shadow seemed to be on a greater, more ominous scale, and he imagined he heard deep, pulse-locked rumblings, the purr of a living engine, the groans of the intelligence that dwelled in the deepest reaches of the lagoon and lorded it over the atoll.

He stayed near the shore, not trusting his endurance. When he swam to the shoreline, no one prevented him from getting out, and as he staggered back to the cottage, there was no trace of the Transparents anywhere.

As he collapsed on the bed, he wondered for just an instant how many days had passed and how many he had left. He'd been here less than a week, and he'd already lost track of time.

And so he adjusted, quickly developing a routine: rise in the morning, eat and then go out to sit at the ocean's edge, looking at that horizon line—so clean and sharp in his imagination but an unfocused haze to his eyes. He would ignore the Transparents entirely during this early morning meditation, though he was always aware of them and the attention they paid to him. Once his breakfast was digested he would begin the regimen that took up a greater and greater part of his day as his strength increased. He would run a third, perhaps halfway, and after awhile all the way around the ring and then dive into the lagoon, swim across to the opposite end and resume the run. As he grew more exhausted, his footing grew worse and he would fall, pounding dangerously at his bones—even his skull—but that wasn't enough to stop him. The promise of the warm, caressing waters of the lagoon seemed to override all concern, as though there was no injury that the lagoon could not heal.

Occasionally he would tread water at the center of the lagoon, turning as he did to take in this new horizon line. From here the view was different: the horizon was no veiled transition of blues, it was a series of jagged slashes between the gentle, unblemished sky and the black, life-choked rocks. This particular horizon line reminded him of something, something doctors had always goaded and prodded him about, but which he had never been comfortable thinking about himself until he'd entered these waters. The doctors had always loved to hear him tell about that moment, had so many questions about the way he told it or the way he hedged around really telling them about it, about Jeremy. But he could still barely share that with himself, let alone with a therapist eager only to get a handle on him, give him the key to maintaining himself with the least amount of effort. But he shared those memories—in silence— with the water, where they made a quiet kind of sense, where he began to realize the benevolent indifference the universe attached to his sins.

He would sleep away the hottest part of the afternoon, or if not, read the woman's journal. None of the other journals were worth the trouble—men's mostly, whiny weaklings in love with their own suffering, for whom the experiences on the atoll seemed to add up to nothing. No doubt many of them hadn't made it. Encrusted in the rocks along the ring he would occasionally find skeletons, and there were probably many more that he wasn't even aware of.

But he wondered ... did any of them ever make it? Did the boat ever really come back?

In the evenings he sat beneath the unwavering moon. It seemed to drift aimlessly across the sky, and though its face seemed to alter subtly from one night to the next, it went through no cycles, remaining full and bright, as though its light-side could not bear to turn away from him.

Every night that single Transparent returned, always sitting on the same rock. Had it begun to take on the characteristics of a she in response to an unstated inner need of his, or because he'd begun referring to it as a she? Seated so elegantly across the rock, her flesh making radiant magic out of the moonlight, her form so perfectly sculpted in what could have only been a response to his own imagination, he sometimes found himself consumed with what in another life he might have called lust. His mouth watered at the sight of her, his eyes teared, his heart and muscles wrenched in hopeless, unappeasable longing. But his penis seemed to have shrunk nearly out of existence during the boat trip out here, and not even the effulgent splendor of his Transparent confessor could coax it out of hiding. So instead, he talked to her. And in his mind, at every pause, she made a perfect response, her voice soft and deep.

What all did he tell her? There was really nothing to tell, was there? Most of his life had been a monotonous routine, his greatest tragedies those of his own making, his most relished victories bitter and pre-emptive strikes against other people. He exaggerated and lied his way through his life, finally realizing that the most enjoyable form of therapy was to either invent something from scratch or switch his own identity with someone to make himself the admirable hero of an anecdote he'd otherwise remembered with bitterness and jealousy. She never questioned or doubted. The perfect audience.

There was nothing you could do.

I would have done the same thing.

How very interesting. Please ... go on.

And then they would go for a swim. He would lose track

of her once they submerged, and she would become just one of many in those pure moonlit waters.

The days were so alike that only two things distinguished them: the entries in the woman's journal he would read on a particular day, and the stories he would tell his Transparent-confessor that night.

Oh ... but there was one other thing. She, his confessor, seemed to be growing larger as the days progressed. He assumed it was a gradual transformation, because he never even noticed at what point she became taller than he. Only a little bit at first, but now it seemed as though she were at least a full head taller, and growing at an ever faster rate.

His few dreams were usually inconsequential—always about people he'd once worked or gone to school with, in neighborhoods he'd lived in as a child. And then, one night, he dreamt of the atoll, of the cottage. Its most immediate distinguishing feature was the absence of the Transparents. As he walked among the rocks, he realized that the atoll was stripped clean, lifeless. The lagoon was dry, and the deep center was now a yawning black pit, the rocks surrounding it gashing a dramatic spiral into its depths. The ocean was reddish-brown, a perfect reflection of the sky. Inside, the cottage was as it must have once been, the furniture gleaming and intact, books on shelves, kitchen and bathroom fully operational, and on a central table in the upstairs room, the computer. His dream self walked up to it, sat down and turned it on. On the screen there appeared a textured surface—rock. There was a coughing, spewing, and blood splattered against that rock while something small and pink bounced against the rock and fell. In the center of that blood-splatter, a perfect stencil in the shape of a hand, its little finger missing. As the red oozed towards the center, the hand retained its shape as it slowly shrank out of existence, an infant's grasping hand, consumed by blood, as the screen hissed and faded to black.

He awoke from that dream just before sunrise, his neck wrenched and his mouth bitter with the taste of blood.

This morning the sun seemed to emerge from the depths of a vast pink tunnel. Concentric arcs billowed over it, and he was at first confused, wondering if perhaps he was still dreaming. It was as though he was inside of something; that this atoll and the ocean were beneath an immense bowl, and the sun was no more than a traveling light, delineating the contours of that bowl.

But of course they were only clouds. He'd almost forgotten what a sunrise could look like on a cloudy day. And of course, it looked just like this. Didn't it?

That night, when he went out and saw her seated upon her rock, he didn't want to talk. No complaints, no lies. He wanted to draw close to her, to lie with his head on her lap, to shut his eyes and forget that he would ever have to leave here, that somehow he would be irrevocably changed and would be dragged off the ring and away from her.

Has anything good ever happened to you? he imagined her asking. *Were you ever truly in love, did you ever have a moment of bliss, give or receive a single tender gesture or word? I dare you to actually remember the best, most beautiful moment in your entire life.*

"The most beautiful moment in my life?" he asked her, though she had said nothing at all to him, and made no indication that she understood or even heard him. "That's funny, because everything good that's ever happened to me sooner or later ended up going bad. I held onto good things until they went bad—until they had no choice but to go bad. If I were to ... Wait. Yeah, I can think of something. Sure I can. This is going to sound stupid, I realize. Inconsequential. But it'll have to do. Okay?"

I'm ready whenever you are.

"Years ago—I was still very young, I'd gone through some very miserable, frustrating experiences ... I'd been despondent for weeks, for months, and suddenly, one day, I just seemed to pull out of it. I was elated simply because I no longer felt depressed. I decided to make a symbolic gesture to myself, to prove to myself that in spite of everything that had been happening to me over the past year, this elation, this boost of confidence was real, not a phase, or as one of my friends so cheerfully put it, that moment of euphoria before I blew my brains out. I chose the most beautiful woman I knew, someone I'd gone to school with who'd just recently moved to the same city I was living in, and I decided to ask her on a date. And so I did. And lo and behold, she said yes.

"I had this friend, a percussionist in a band. I had no idea what kind of music they played, but he told me they were giving an outdoor concert in the mountains in a couple of weeks. Why not bring her to that? It seemed like a reasonable idea.

"It was really pathetic the way I prepared for that, so meticulously planned out every detail, drove every one of my friends nuts asking for advice and then turning around and explaining to them exactly how it was going to be. Everything was so perfectly crystallized in my imagination there didn't even really seem much point in tainting the experience with the real thing.

"But finally the day came. Well, first of all, she was new in this part of the country. She'd come from out east, where we'd gone to school. The altitude at city level was still aggravating to her. And now here we were, driving mountain roads, climbing mountain stairways to this cliff-side band shell, and she could barely breathe. Well, she was exhausted and really pissed off by the time we made it, and by then the crowds were huge. It was cold and there was nowhere left to sit. We had to stand. When I told her I knew someone in the band she just scowled and looked away.

"And the music! Jesus, they were loud. Loads of percussion, grating machine noise, and just about the most insane rasping vocals I'd ever heard. Under other circumstances I think I might have liked it, but she hated it. I wished the concert had been after dark so that I wouldn't have had to read her distaste so clearly. And the audience was full of agitators, peripherals of the band I guess, shooting water jets, fireworks, whipping around flaming torches. It was insane. Finally, some kid right next to us, a boy about seventeen, got his hair caught on fire. Well, that was it. She went nuts. I had to get her out of there, she was so scared and pissed and disgusted.

"But instead of going back down to my car, we walked to a picnic area and sat for awhile. It was snowing now, coming down pretty hard. And yet it wasn't that cold or windy. It was actually very pleasant. I knew the date was a bust and that, if I stopped long enough to think about it, I'd see that this whole experience was just more proof of the same hopeless stupidity that had plagued everything else that I'd done all year. But we talked, reminisced about school, talked about our lives—our very distinct and never to be intersected lives—and just ... talked. We sat in a gazebo for about an hour like that, and at the end of it, I guess we both felt a little better. We got up to leave and then, when we were about fifty feet from the gazebo, she stopped and I stopped and we talked some more and I apologized for bringing her to this stupid concert. She shrugged it off so beautifully, as if to say it wasn't your fault, I had a nice time just knowing you wanted me to have a good time. God ... And the snow was falling around us and I looked at the gazebo over her right shoulder, and I looked at her and ...

"Snow was collecting in her hair, melting on her nose and cheeks. There, on her long ... perfect eyelashes, snowflakes were collecting, clinging. It gave her face a kind of ... I don't know. Radiance doesn't seem to do it justice. And in that moment I saw her as she would look in twenty, thirty years, still just as beautiful, standing in this same spot, her hair gray, her face etched and wrinkled, snow falling around her, snowflakes still searching out and clinging to those gorgeous, sweeping eyelashes."

He laughed and threw a stone into the ocean. "I'll never forget that moment—and I'm not even sure why. If I forget everything else that's ever happened to me, even if I forget who she was, I'll still cling to that one vision. Stupid, isn't it? So stupid I've never even said it out loud before."

Did you ever see her again? he imagined his confessor asking.

"No. I had to leave that city soon afterward, and all my inconsequential fantasies leading up to that date, all the friends I'd driven crazy yapping about it ... they just disappeared from my life."

He'd been looking out at the ocean, at the haze around the moon. He turned to her now and found her standing, something stern and menacing in her bearing.

"What?" he asked, looking up at her. She was at least ten feet tall. She turned away and marched towards the lagoon. When she was up to her knees and he reached the shoreline, she turned and held out an obstructing arm.

"Don't go. Not yet. I want to talk some more."

He took one step forward and she struck him across the face with an open palm. He fell against the rocks, his wrenched neck suddenly throbbing with pain so intense he was sure it was broken. Slowly, trying in vain to minimize that pain, he stood. She was gone.

He slept little that night, in fits and bursts, while the pain got worse, and then, towards dawn, began to ease up. Finally, at sunrise, he fell into a deep sleep that held him under for several hours. It was the buzzing that woke him this time. He sat up screaming, but there was nothing there.

The air was cool that morning; tendrils of cold whipped across the rocks, whistling, shrieking past his ear. He returned to the cottage twice to layer his clothing a little more, and each time it seemed a little colder than before. The eastern horizon looked as though it had hemorrhaged gray-black blood, darkening sky and ocean and spreading as he watched.

The ocean had just come to life. That storm ... it reminded him of something. What? His whole life he'd had a talent for losing himself in the suggested images in clouds. What did he see now? Was that a face, a cluster of smashed faces, a body crushed upon the rocks, a crowded insect hive?

No ... It was a brain, convolutions twisting into ever tighter, labyrinthine patterns, expanding to fill that bowl that was the sky above him. Jesus Christ, he realized, this island ... this dainty little ring of rock is about to be wiped clean. And me with it! He'd never seen a storm approach so quickly, rolling in on itself as it rose, separating into innumerable lobes. Oh, he had no doubt. This thing could think. How could it not?

Great fish leaped out of the water, a glistening whale with what appeared to be gigantic feathers growing out of its flank broke the surface to let out a single agonizing scream before gravity pulled it back under.

The rocks were almost deserted, except for thousands of

annoying white fist-sized worms that had at one time been only a marginal denizen, food for the sea birds. Now they were everywhere, impervious to the cold and the raging sea water. He tried to avoid them as he made his way back towards the cottage, but they were impossible not to step on, and impossible to get any footing on. The only safe way of moving now, with the wind so powerful, was to go on his hands and knees, but that would have meant touching them, looking at them from just an arm's length away. He had to walk, and yet it was not possible.

He was on a vulnerable peak when the wave hit him and carried him into the lagoon. With the sweatshirts and vest it was hard to swim in this suddenly turbulent water, especially as the wind and the invading seawater drove him further and further towards the center of the lagoon. At least the water here was warm, at least thirty degrees warmer than the air. He pulled off the vest, let it float away, and tried to conquer the turbulence by swimming through it. This lagoon had been good to him, it was warming him in the wake of the approaching storm—it would buffet him, and those who lived down there would surely never let him drown.

He was being blown towards the far shore, away from the cottage. He fought against the waves and the rain, but it was all he could do to keep from being pulled under entirely.

The wind and water hurled him onto the rocks. He crawled on his belly, never mind the worms, trying only to keep from being thrown into the ocean or back into the lagoon.

He looked up into the sky and screamed, "I want my money back!" and then plunged through the underbrush, head first into a pit of rising water. He found a perch and settled securely into a depression in the rock.

So familiar … What was it? He wiped the slime away from his body in the darkness, and felt the tough shards within that slime scrape at his clothes and skin. What was so familiar about this? The thunder, the torrents of water … no, it was something else, clinging to his skin, clinging to those rocks. And it was the buzzing. It took him a long time to distinguish that sound, but once he did, it was impossible to mistake it for anything else.

He scooped away a crushed white worm from beneath him and held it in front of his face, trying to catch just the barest outline of it in the darkness. No use. But he could feel it. Armored, segmented legs, struggling out of a larval goo, the needled tip of its abdomen tapping against his palm.

He screamed and tried to flick it away. The slime flew off, but the thing within it—oh, he knew what it was—remained. He let out another scream, and this was all the prompting it needed to plunge the stinger deep into his palm.

And then, they began swarming, hovering, diving, perching on him and creeping into his clothes, stinging him over and over, exactly as they had that day, only now it was dark and he was alone. There was no one here for him, just as there might as well not have been anyone there for Jeremy, and the whole thing came flooding back to him now. Not the detached, well-rehearsed story he'd been forced to tell a hundred times, but the terror and the burning pain, the ferocity of the damned insects, that hopeless assurance that no one was going to come, no one was going to pull him out of this one. It was only him, and he could do nothing. He resigned himself to it and let himself die. Or so he hoped.

It was the sunlight that woke him, a shaft of light pouring through an opening only a few feet and a safe crawl away from where he had huddled through most of the storm. The wasps, or whatever the hell they'd been, were gone. They'd emerged out of the innocuous worms he'd been seeing on the rocks ever since his arrival. Jesus, they'd been there at his feet the whole time, just waiting.

The atoll was stripped clean, a ring of featureless rock. The lagoon was sealed shut by a translucent membrane, thin but impenetrable, its surface laced with innumerable strands and vessels of red and blue. He crawled out onto that membrane, because the air was still cold, the membrane warm, and the movement of fluids within its vessels gave a sadly familiar aura to this now barren and dismal world. The sky was gray, the sun could have been anywhere, and he could not escape even for a moment into that warm, safe water. Could not rupture the membrane.

Spread beneath its surface he saw two disintegrating sheets of paper and an embroidered notebook cover. He'd unsealed that woman's journal and left it for the elements to destroy.

He'd always thought that if his provisions were to fail him, he would scavenge from the rocks, if the Transparents were ever to desert him he would have the notebook and its passionate confessions to keep him company. But he had none of that now.

He called out to them. To her. He knew they were down there somewhere—or maybe they were the membrane itself. Yeah, that made sense. Was that the pressure of gas erupting beneath the surface making the membrane roll and ripple like that, or was it the subsumed Transparents, now a single organism, breathing? He pressed against it, trying to reach around it, pull it nearer, enwrap himself in it, but there was a definite resistance there. It wanted no part of him.

The membrane sent ripples, pushing him, lifting him and throwing him towards the shoreline, until he was hurled onto the rocks.

He was still there when darkness finally spanned the sky and the moon appeared, a dull sliver glowing behind the clouds. *Why am I not dead yet?* he wondered. *The forty days are never going to end or else they ended a long time ago and no one is ever coming to get me or they were coming to get me and the storm blew them off course or pounded them into the ocean. Why ... Why did I ask for this? Why couldn't I have committed myself or killed myself or worse yet, just gone on with my life? Found a new place to live in a new city, found a new companion for myself, a new livelihood? What is penance anyway? When the crime is just the corrosion of my own soul, the awareness that the good in me is dead and has been dead for a long, long time ...*

He staggered to the edge of the lagoon, and began walking along the shoreline. Surely by the time he made it around once, something would happen. Surely by then, if he called to them, if he reminded them he was here, they would return. She would return, and listen. This time he would tell the truth.

"You never let me finish, you know," he cried. The only reply was the gentle undulation of the membrane. "You realize

almost everything I ever told you was a bunch of shit. Lies ...
All that crap about people wronging me or mistreating me or
not appreciating me. None of that was real. No one ever really
did anything too bad to me. The worst thing anyone ever did
to me was see the truth. The real me. And you know what that
is? I've never done a single thing in my entire life, never raised
a finger to help anyone, never had a decent thing to say to
anyone ... Nothing. I've led a monumentally worthless life. You
know the boldest thing I've ever done? Turn myself in to your
employers. Sacrifice everything I ever had or would ever have
just so I could punish myself. Here! And for what? "

But that wasn't it, was it? That was always the cushion, the
padding, the scar tissue, with which he secluded and cradled
... the Memory.

"Okay. I did do one thing. Once. Hear me out there? I did
do one thing! It's on all my charts! I told you the best thing that
ever happened to me, the most beautiful moment in my life,
remember? And it was so trivial I'd never had the guts to say it
to a real human being. But the worst moment of my life? Jesus,
everybody I've ever known knows something about it. Since it's
the only thing that's ever happened to me, it's all the doctors
ever wanted to talk about. I've told it a million times and I
figured that I could get here and my suffering would be so great
that finally, I wouldn't have to say anything about it anymore.
But I was wrong. I have to talk. I can't stop talking. And if I have
only one thing to say, then I guess I just go through my whole
life, telling that same thing over and over and over again. Fine!
Okay? Ready?"

He stood on a rise, cupped his hands around his mouth.
"I was a cub scout! Can you believe that? I was a fucking cub
scout! Me ... and Jeremy. He was my best friend. He joined the
cub scouts because I did, just so we could be together, compete
to see who could get all those shitty little arrowhead patches the
fastest." He stopped and took a deep breath. "But I don't mean
to say it like that. We were snotty little brats, we were just the
kind of kids that I would never be able to put up with now. Too
hard to maintain, too loud and energetic and ... out of control.
But that was ... I think ... the way we were supposed to be.

To have been anything less than that then would mean that I'd have been the way I am now for my entire life. At least I was a colossal pain in the ass when I was a kid. Considering all the dullards I've met in the world, to have been that wild and ... alive, that was a real accomplishment.

"Anyway ... Jeremy and I were cub scouts. One year we all took a trip down to a state park, with cliffs and a man-made lake and a man-made waterfall ... a very cool place. We were there just for the day. No real provisions, no real supervision, only a few dullard parents to keep an eye on us. We weren't supposed to wander off. You know, we were supposed to be 'good.' I mean, they take a bunch of eight-, nine-, ten-year-old suburban kids into a place like that and tell us to behave in an orderly fashion. Idiots. And of course they were our parents or our friend's parents, so we tried to listen to them, but it was impossible. A bunch of us were at the top of this cliff, and out on the edge there was this cactus in bloom. This was about as far north as you'll ever see a wild cactus, and none of us had ever seen one before. We decided to pick it. I crept out to the edge of the cliff, but it was already sloping downwards, I was losing my footing and I still couldn't reach the thing. I gave up. No one else even got as far as I did. But Jeremy, he was always a little bit crazier than the rest of us, and those last two feet I hadn't had the guts to creep, he did, and he managed to reach the cactus. And he gave it a good hard yank, thinking, I guess, that the thing must have been rooted pretty securely there. Which it wasn't. It came up like nothing at all, and Jeremy hadn't expected that. He lost his balance, started to slide, turned back to us, reaching out—for one of us, for a plant, anything to grab onto but there was nothing there and besides, he was only grabbing with one hand because he wouldn't let go of the damn cactus. He didn't even shout at first because he was just sliding and I think he must have thought he'd catch himself before he fell too far. When he screamed, we knew.

"We ran down a nearby slope to get a look at him. He'd fallen onto a ledge about forty feet down. He was hurt but when we called out to him he answered. He was conscious. He knew what was going on, but he was hurting. And ... there was something else wrong. He was calling out for help in a way that meant he was worried about more than just getting off the ledge.

"I panicked. What the hell was wrong with Jeremy? We couldn't leave him there like that. I told the other guys to go get the adults, because it was obvious we were never going to get out of this without getting them involved and getting our asses kicked for it later. But I couldn't get to him from downslope like this. There didn't seem to be any way of getting to him ... except to go over and make the same fall he did. Like I could do it and not get hurt.

"But see ... I did it. I ran back up there and, without even thinking about it, I went right over that cliff, sliding downslope almost the whole way. I don't know how I did it. I was like a ... I don't know ... spiderboy or something. Anyway, here I come, I can see the free fall ahead and I see Jeremy right under me, right on the edge and I shout out to him, 'Out of the way, stupid!' He looks up, sees me falling, catches the landslide I'm bringing with me and rolls out of the way.

"And that's when the screams really started. I landed on that ledge feet first. Wrenched my ankle a little, but otherwise, perfect. But Jeremy's screaming. I look at him. He's rolled to the very back of the ledge, right into the wasps. Jesus, they were all over him. And he's screaming 'Get 'em off me! Get 'em off me!' and I'm still not thinking. I have no fear of anything at this point, so I grab him and pull him away from the swarm, and of course, the swarm follows him. Now they're swarming both of us. We're swatting at them, screaming, trying to kill them or scare them away but they just keep on coming. And that buzzing ... it sounded like laughter, like they were really enjoying themselves. I don't remember how many times I got stung before they finally quit. Way, way too many times, but not half as many times as Jeremy. I'm feeling awful, but Jeremy, he's really sick. He's getting sicker by the moment. I find a spot away from the edge and away from the wasps and I drag him over there, try to sit him up, try not to panic, try to talk to him, but Jeremy ... something's going very wrong here. His tongue is growing, his eyes are turning red and bulging and his breathing is getting bad. And he's afraid he's dying. But of course he's not dying. Everybody gets stung by wasps, don't they? I mean, sure, there were a lot of them, but how could he die? He survived a fall like this, and to die because a bunch of bugs stung him? What kind of bullshit is that? So I try to sit him up, but he won't sit. He can't. He's lying down and he's shivering and he's calling out to his mom, and shit, his mom is a hundred miles away and our scout leader doesn't even like him very much and Jeremy's reaching out for someone and I'm the only one there. He grabs a hold of me and I grab a hold of him and he just lies there, his head in my lap, looking out at the edge, waiting for the adults to come rescue us. And oh, God, he's looking worse, sounding worse by the minute. Choking. And he *is* dying. He's fucking allergic to the little bastards. And he's dying and he's looking up at me and he's begging me not to let him die and he's telling me to get his mom and asking me 'When are they going to get here?' and then ... I can't understand him at all.

"They had to get the rangers—or whatever they were—to rappel down to us. I guess it must have taken a long time to find them, I don't know. But I was watching the sky change color over the edge of the cliff ledge. It was like the edge of the world, and beyond it, everything was just getting darker and darker. He was long dead by the time they got to us. I'd been talking to him the whole time. See ... I'd been too stunned or too embarrassed to answer him, console him while he was babbling to me but now that he was dead I couldn't stop talking to him. And I wouldn't let go of him."

He laughed, stepped off the rock and continued to walk around the lagoon. "They tried to pry him away from me, and I wouldn't let them do it. I don't know ... I was too freaked out to know what I was doing. I was ten years old for chrissakes. When one guy tried to grab me and pull me away, I bit him. I bit down on his little finger. *I bit his little finger off.* I used to tell the doctors that I bit it off and then spit it in his face but I probably made that part up.

"But anyway, that's it. My big, valiant moment of glory, and it turned out to be the worst moment in my whole life. How do you make up for something like that? Jeremy wouldn't have even joined the cub scouts if it hadn't been for me, he wouldn't have had to get that cactus if I could have gotten it and he wouldn't have rolled into that wasp's nest if I hadn't decided to go down there and 'rescue' him myself.

"You know, sometimes, I think about that day, trying to look at it from every angle and trying to figure out what I did wrong, what I could have done right, trying to find some kind of useful lesson in there, but there's nothing. Just this: sometimes I run it all through my head and I end up thinking, 'Well, at least I bit that asshole's finger off.'

"And that's IT."

No reply from the sealed lagoon. They knew better. The only cure for him was the immemorial one—annihilation. And that was just what they had prescribed for him. Annihilation. He could see his end so clearly now.

He collapsed on the rocks, a dramatic swirl with arms out to his side, as though uniformed attendants would break his fall, catch him and set him gently in a bed. But no one caught him. He hit the rocks and all the wounds that the lagoon water had washed away with its magic—in the feet and elbows and knees, in his skull—all returned now. He was hungry. He was cold. What was left of the cottage was halfway around the atoll and he didn't think he could even remember how to stand, let alone walk.

So he didn't.

When the sun rose the next morning the sky was clearing. He could see it. He could feel himself on the rocks and wondered when he would finally decide to move. But the hours passed, the sun glared down on him, and he did not feel the inclination to move. There was such a security in being so immobile, in fitting—molding into the rocks so snugly, and he began to wonder if perhaps he was only imagining the hunger and thirst and that, in reality, he was dead, and that, if he tried to move and couldn't, and then realized he was dead, he would panic. So he didn't try. He felt random sensations: heat, the pressure of the rocks beneath him, but no pain of any kind. It was all he could do to remember where he was and why he was here and why it should even matter whether he did remember. When night came again, and he had gone an entire day without moving, he looked upon it as a kind of victory.

In another day life began to creep out of the lagoon and out of the ocean and claim territories on the atoll. The plants reasserted themselves and the fresh and saltwater creatures began battling for dominance. But he paid no attention to this. He was nothing more than a part of the territory the plants and animals were laying claim to; first the creepers and mosses and worms and bugs, then the crabs from the ocean and the primeval arthropods from the lagoon began to claim niches for themselves on his body. By the end of the third day, he seemed to be growing into the rock.

A part of him was aware of the war for dominance being waged on him, but seldom and then only vaguely. It was then not so much the degradation he was suffering that bothered him as the fact that he was still aware of it—or of anything at all. And then he would fade away, sometimes thinking that perhaps these were not the thoughts of a man, but the thoughts of a mineral, that he was and had always been a rock, only now awakening from a nightmare in which he had been a brittle, disposable vessel of flesh and blood.

On the fifth day, as the plants began to anchor and hide him and the tiny animals ran rampant over him, as dehydration began to reach critical levels, the membrane across the lagoon began to break apart. Within hours it was gone, all its constituent parts broken down into organisms no larger than a child's thumbnail, each one transparent with threads of crimson and blue dancing within. Some began creeping ashore in an orderly procession, covering his body and slipping into his mouth, where they would secrete fresh water directly into his throat, while others spread across the flesh to protect the old wounds and seal the new ones. The tiny Transparents held vigil on him for the next ten days, at which point a boat whistle sounded out on the ocean, and a small craft approached the atoll, and a young man and woman got out and began calling to him in a name he would have no longer recognized had he been conscious enough to hear it.

It took them, and finally three others as well, half the day to find the body. This trip out they had recovered three live ones out of over a dozen scheduled pick-ups. For the rest, the pilgrimage had been a very expensive, slow and probably tortuous form of suicide. For those three who'd survived ... who could say? It wasn't the crew's job to bother with that kind of stuff.

She had been the last one to speak to him before the boat had taken off forty days ago. He'd stood on the rocks watching them, looking confused, as though he had no clear idea of what was happening to him, as though someone else had planned this for him, had drugged and shanghaied him. She'd felt worse for him than for most others, because he seemed less pathetic, less despicable than so many of the others she'd seen. To think that he was lost, he of all of them, was almost too much. Long after they'd dragged the lagoon and the rest had wanted to give up the search, she continued searching the rock formations.

And so she was the one who first saw his hand, withered and pale, hanging out of a mass of tangles in a recess among the rocks. They spent the next hour pulling the plants away, scooping away the colonies of things living on him, only to discover that he was virtually lodged to the rocks. The slime covering him made it impossible to get a grip on him and it seemed for a while that they would have to chip him away and drag him back to the boat with twenty pounds of rock imbedded in his flesh. But with the plants gone and the skin exposed to the sunlight, the slime melted away and they were finally able to pull him cleanly away.

He let out a scream when they got him to his feet, and began to cry furiously, though without ever opening his eyes or thrashing those scabbed, emaciated limbs.

The Transparents began to resonate the moment they heard his cries— resonate and merge, climbing and rolling over the terrain to watch the little boat and its howling passenger meet up with the larger boat and then drift away, towards the horizon line. Then the Transparents slipped back into the center depths of the lagoon.

He slept for three days, while he was cleaned and pumped full of drugs and fed intravenously. Towards the end of that sleep he had a dream: he was in this very bed, awake and alert as the room was overrun by grime-encrusted demons who dragged him out of bed, beat a hole through the floor with their hammers, and hauled him through the opening and into the underworld, so crowded with demons that the very cliff walls seemed to be composed of them. He was dragged into a dark room deep, deep within the earth, his head laid out on an iron slab. There they crushed his head with repeated blows of the hammers. He actually watched it from near the ceiling of the room, his floating spirit bobbing quietly lest the demons impacted in that ceiling should notice him. A bleached white skull was laid out on the slab, so pure and unmarked it looked as though it had been freshly molded. The liquified flesh that puddled around the shards of the crushed skull now drifted across the slab and crept up the new one, where it began to hiss and effervesce. He was held up by two demons while two others twisted the new head onto the shoulders and then threw the whole twitching mess into a stream of bloodied water that had now appeared, running down the center of the room, over a ledge and into a great wet darkness …

… He was standing in the snow, on a level stretch halfway up a mountain, shivering cold. His head hurt so badly in so many places that he could think of nothing but the demons' hammers. Then he realized that it was the newness of his skull that pained him so much, and that when he opened and shut his mouth, his muscles were teaching the jawbone how to move. He could hear the buzzing—could see the wasps swarming in the treetops not far away

"Don't be afraid of them," she said. He turned slowly, recognizing the voice but unable to place it until he set eyes on the young woman he had brought to this mountain some fifteen years before. He was disappointed—he'd been hoping it would be his Transparent-confessor. There, over the woman's shoulder, was that same gazebo, more rundown than before, and she too was older, far older than she should have been, and far different from what he'd envisioned on that day.

He stared at her, waiting for a word, a smile. But her expression was sad until her eyes roamed and she spotted something behind him. She nodded. "Don't look at me," she said softly, "look over there."

And so he turned, afraid that the sound swelling behind him was the swarming wasps, but as his eyes scanned the mountainside, it seemed to be eroding, hazing over, until finally it became the ocean, a calm, dark blue ocean with a horizon line that slashed across the much-lighter sky. And as he turned further, the sky darkened, the ocean lightened, the horizon line diffused until all he could see was a soft blue oblivion.

"Here he comes now," said the voice. It was not the dream voice; it was higher pitched, almost a young girl's voice. The oblivion was not so soft anymore. Everywhere, that white glare, and moving within it, an unfocused face—blond haired and blue-eyed and, just possibly, familiar.

"Good morning. Can you hear me all right?" He could feel her breath against his face. She drew closer now. "Nod or speak, whichever's easier." He was aware of doing something, but he was still too unformed to recognize whether he'd said a word or merely moved his head.

"That's good. You're on the boat. The same boat. I was the one who dropped you off, remember? I'm the one who found you ... It's okay if you don't remember. You were ... really sick ... but you're better now."

Another movement from him. He recognized it: expelled air, molded by the larynx and tongue, buzzing between his lips.

She drew even closer now, and he could feel her hair against his cheeks. "Your name is Jeremy now. Can you understand that? That's your name. Can you say Jeremy? "

He swallowed and struggled with his lips. "Bu-badda-ba."

"Very good," she purred. "That's very good. We're going to have you up and walking in the next day or two. Won't that be nice? We're going to work on your new signature then."

He turned and looked at the rest of the room. A bare, ugly room glaring with white light. On the wall, a porthole, a window on a ship's cabin. The glass revealed nothing except the reflection of room light. He looked back at the face, only a few inches above his now. She was smiling at him. No, he had never seen her before. He would have remembered her.

"And then," she said, her voice clipped as she stood straight and backed away from him, "we're going to have to do some paperwork."

And with that she opened the cabin door to walk out of the room. He couldn't find the strength or even the words to call her back. *Please don't go. Stay and talk to me. Tell me who I am. Don't leave. Not yet.* He turned away wincing as the door swung shut. He was looking at the glare on the porthole glass when he heard the click on the wall outside the cabin and the room light shut off. The glare disappeared from the glass, and he could see the clear, perfect blue of the sky, small and out of reach.

From the vantage point of the ship's deck, the sky was almost totally clear, its only blemish a lone cumulus cloud, drifting on the westerlies at an altitude of 6,000 feet. Within those glowing billows of water droplets, shadows deepened and dimmed in complex patterns. To look carefully at that cloud, one might have seen faces—dead, swollen faces; young faces of flawless beauty; ancient, all knowing faces—or perhaps a menagerie of animals, the twisted wreckage of ancient machines, rock formations, or bold sweeps of light and darkness that conveyed dread and love and crippling hesitation and the exhilaration of having waited an eternity to take possession of the trillions of cells that it was now turn to call your own.

But Jeremy, wired, tubed and strapped to his bed, couldn't see any of that.

Not yet.

The Story of Jeffrey Osier

Jeffrey Osier was born in Chicago Illinois in 1954, on the very day that a CIA covert operation brought down the government of Guatemala. His very first movie theater experience was George Pal's *Tom Thumb*. His very first musical hero was Bernard Herrmann. His first phase of short story writing dealt mainly with the effects of radiation on insects and the awakening of great slumbering dinosaurs. This was followed by a series of stories dealing mainly with the fact that girls didn't like him. This was followed by … oh, what's the use. Listen … he's a dabbler, pure and simple. He plays various musical instruments, sometimes; draws and paints, sometimes; and writes short stories, sometime in the past. He is married to the exceptionally wonderful Cathy VanPatten, has two amazing children, one grandchild, and two cats.

He is currently working on a very important project whose details he is keeping under wraps just in case he never finishes it.

Curious about other Crossroad Press books?
Stop by our site:
http://store.crossroadpress.com
We offer quality writing
in digital, audio, and print formats.

Enter the code FIRSTBOOK
to get 20% off your first order from our store!
Stop by today!